Mind Hacking Happiness

Volume I:

The Quickest Way to Happiness and Controlling Your Mind

by Sean Webb

Contact Info:

sean@mindhackinghappiness.com

To my wife and son

Thanks to everyone mentioned in this book for your personal advice, guidance, scientific research, stories and support.

And special thanks to George Cornelius who caught a ton of my mistakes.

ALL IS FAERIE IN LOVE AND WAR

ISLA FROST

Copyright © 2021 by Isla Frost
All rights reserved.

Published by JFP Trust
2021 First Print Edition

ISBN: 978 1 922712 05 9

www.islafrost.com

WHAT YOU OUGHT TO KNOW
ABOUT LYRA'S WORLD

In the fifty years prior to the magic revolution, tech advanced in the vigorous leaps and bounds of a newly hatched dragon, and the human population doubled from four to eight billion—forcing the supernaturals to become more and more restricted in their mandate to stay hidden.

They decided enough was enough.

But they didn't just book a tell-all slot on *Oprah*. First they came together in an unprecedented display of cooperation and inflicted—or gifted depending who you listened to—humankind with magic.

As an opening move, arming your potential adversary with brand-new power is a counterintuitive way to go. But it worked. Sort of.

Making everyone magical leveled the playing field somewhat. And arming every idiot in the world with magic abilities gave humankind something more immediate to fear than the seemingly well-behaved supernaturals. Especially with all the positive press about the heroic soldiers, doctors, firefighters, and social workers who'd been living among us all along.

It came out later that they'd carefully bought up key media outlets before pulling the trigger on their plan so they could massage the reactions of the masses. They spun the magic revolution as their gift to the world. Some conspiracy theorists even claimed they'd orchestrated the Harry Potter phenomenon to ensure humankind would accept it as such.

Even so, for the governments, those early days were like an impossible game of Whac-A-Mole. But most of the world survived.

This story is set in a city that didn't.

Las Vegas was one of a few places to be razed to the ground during the transition period. Turns out the people that frequent Sin City are not the safest people to give magical powers to.

Miraculously, or more specifically, thanks to the hard work of the gold-loving goblins who'd had their sights on the casinos for decades, only a few people died. And a new Las Vegas was built in its place. A Las Vegas that catered to all species, establishing it as one of the most diverse and integrated cities in the world.

It's been smooth sailing ever since.

Ha.

CHAPTER ONE

I approached the residential home with my dragon partner Aurelis huffing down my neck.

This was one of her least favorite duties.

Most of our jobs within the Rapid Response unit of the LVMPD were dealing with a dangerous situation already in progress. We were there to protect lives, contain the perpetrators, and minimize the fallout. But this call was preemptive—on mere suspicion of brewing trouble. Which meant more talking on our part and sometimes a wasted trip altogether.

Hence Aurelis's bad mood.

I, on the other hand, was just happy to be on duty again. It was my first day back at work after two weeks' suspension.

"I've missed you breathing down my neck," I told her sunnily.

The next breath had more heat in it. And a hint of smoke.

A warning I ignored.

But only thanks to months of practice. The majestic copper-scaled dragon following me down the footpath was terrifying on a primordial level that took all my willpower to overcome. She was stronger, faster, and smarter than me, and her design was pure predator. Lethal talons tipped each of her feet, wicked horns adorned her head and neck, and her powerful maw bristled with teeth made for tearing flesh—on display even when her jaw was closed. A twenty-foot wingspan and magical mastery over the air itself meant her prey had little hope of escape. And once you were caught—if you survived long enough to realize it—her armor of interlocking scales and natural magic resistance rendered her impervious to most methods of defense. And just in case all that wasn't enough, as the smoke insinuated, she breathed freaking *fire*.

There was a reason that of all the supernatural creatures that had gone into hiding around the globe, dragons had remained so deeply embedded in the human psyche. But this particular dragon had saved my ass on more than one occasion, visited me in the hospital, and even loaned me one of the books from her precious hoard, so I was *pretty* sure she wouldn't decide to eat me just for irking her.

The suspect's home was perfectly innocuous for the nicer suburb of Goblin Ridge, Las Vegas. A two-story building in desert-inspired colors with a swimming pool and double garage on a generous-sized block.

Perfectly innocuous that is, except for the very real armored tank sitting by the curb.

I rang the doorbell. There was one of those *THIS HOME IS PROTECTED BY GOD AND GUNS* signs stuck in the window, and I snorted. If you had a tank out the front, you didn't need a sign.

Aurelis pushed off behind me and alighted on the roof. Ostensibly to keep a lookout but more likely just to avoid dealing with the pesky occupants.

I didn't mind. Having an ancient predator of myth and flame looming over your shoulder was useful for a lot of things, but in my experience, convincing a person to stay calm and talk wasn't one of them.

Some of the shingles shifted beneath her weight, and I hoped she wouldn't do more damage than we'd been sent to prevent.

In the days following the terror and chaos of Las Vegas's population being imprisoned and held hostage, the city had been quiet. Residents were shaken, and many supernaturals were still regaining their strength after brushing shoulders with Death. Which was perhaps why we'd been assigned to this less-than-critical job.

Well, that and of all the officers in our precinct, Aurelis was best suited to take on a tank.

The quiet wouldn't last. It never did in Vegas. The casinos were putting on star-riddled special events to tempt the tourists into venturing back. We were ten days out from hosting this year's G23 summit. The jinn would soon be holding their annual Grant a Wish charity auction. And in the great words of Albert Einstein: *Two things are infinite: the universe and human stupidity; and I'm not sure about the universe.*

The door opened. "About time you showed up, you useless—"

The man choked off mid-diatribe when he caught sight of my LVMPD uniform.

"Good morning, sir—"

He slammed the door in my face.

I sighed. Aurelis snickered.

I took a couple of steps to one side. Just in case he'd gone to grab one of the guns the sign warned about and take a potshot at me through the door.

The suspect, a Mr. Vargas, did in fact legally own the retired military tank as part of his Adventure Shooting business, promising tourists an explosively good time. He even had the special effects magic to match— ensuring they were the dramatic dark-smoke-and-billow-ing-fireball kinds of explosions customers expected from movies rather than the unsatisfyingly efficient reality. But his permit for the tank did not extend to bringing it into the metro area.

I shifted one hand to the Taser at my hip and rang the doorbell again. My newly acquired chain magic was more versatile than the Taser. But while I'd longed for a power like that my whole life, I was worried this might be one of those careful-what-you-wish-for scenarios. Until I had a chance to ascertain whether Stewie's suppositions were based on paranoia or fact, whether using this magic might attract undesirable and even dangerous attention, I was playing it safe and not using it where I might be seen. I'd gone twenty-two years of my life without a self-sufficient magic ability, so it shouldn't be much of a hardship. Not to mention the *way* I'd acquired it still made me queasy.

To my surprise, the door swung open again.

"Sorry about that," Mr. Vargas said. "I just had to get something off the stove."

I gave him my best don't-mess-with-me gaze. Something that would've been easier to pull off if I wasn't younger than his two daughters. The fact I had to look *up* at him to do it, combined with my blue eyes, brown curls, and a face that tended toward "approachable" even when I was fantasizing about punching someone, didn't help my cause. "Is that so?"

He nodded. But his eyes flicked around like he was nervous. Which didn't suit the grizzled-veteran look he had oozing from every weathered pore.

The thing was, Mr. Vargas didn't have anything worse on his record than a couple of speeding tickets. I wasn't expecting this to end up in a mini-war reenactment. But a fully functional armored tank in the most populated city of Nevada warranted investigation.

"Mr. Vargas, why is there a tank in front of your house?"

"I own it."

"Yes," I said patiently. "But your permit only applies to your private rural property fifty miles away. Why is it *here?*"

"It needed a wash."

I raised an eyebrow. "So why not wash it on-site?"

"I have to pay twice as much to get someone out there."

I closed my eyes for a moment to gather additional patience, then remembered this guy's propensity for guns and snapped them open again. "I'm certain the cost of driving the tank into the city is less than the cost of having someone come out to your property. What's really going on, Mr. Vargas? If you had a valid reason for bringing it here, you should have applied for a special permit."

He folded his arms, and this time his twitchy gaze landed on me and stayed there. "A permit? Do you *know* how much paperwork I have to do every year to run my business? It's my vehicle. I should be able to drive it where I want without begging and scraping and wasting away my life on a bunch of bullshit red tape and money-grabbing schemes set up by the government."

My own hatred of paperwork made me sympathize. If I made the wrong call here and something went wrong, I'd be able to drown myself in a stack of the stuff like Scrooge McDuck and his money pit. But I did not allow my expression to soften.

"I understand your frustration, but—"

My comm chimed in my ear. "Unit Twenty-Seven, we've got a new job for you."

I frowned at Mr. Vargas. "Excuse me a moment." Then I half turned and touched the button on my wrist that would send audio through to dispatch. "The last call is still in progress," I murmured. "Can't you send someone else?"

"A kid's threatening to jump off a cell tower and has asked for you personally, Ridley. Unless there's extreme and imminent danger in your current job, it can wait."

A million questions raced through my mind, but the one I asked was, "Who's the kid?"

"I'll fill you in when you're en route. I've already sent you the location."

I turned back to Vargas. "I have to go. But this matter hasn't been resolved. Please don't relocate your tank again until the LVMPD gives you the go-ahead."

He grunted and shut the door in my face. Again.

Fear for the waiting kid warred with unease that something fishy was going on here.

Aurelis hopped down onto the driveway.

"You don't happen to know how to disable a tank in a few seconds flat, do you?" I asked.

She rolled a slitted golden eye toward me. "Sure. The military made them super easy to tamper with."

Of all the human relational practices she could've picked up on, I wished sarcasm wasn't the one she'd mastered.

7

"What about the main gun?" I persisted, using her knee as a launchpad to scramble onto her shoulders.

"Leave it, Lyra. If it makes you feel better, that tank represents only a fraction of the total firepower in Vegas."

It did not make me feel better. But I shoved the motorcycle helmet over my head and prepared for takeoff.

No, the helmet hadn't been designed with dragon flight in mind, but neither had my human body. It had only taken a half dozen insects lodging themselves in my tonsils for me to decide helmet hair was a reasonable exchange for bug protection.

I tapped my comm again. "We're en route. What's the story?"

"We don't have much to go on yet. The person who called it in said there's a kid between the ages of eight and twelve up in a cell tower. Dark hair. Dark clothes. Too far away to see details. But he's asking for you and threatening to jump if anyone else gets close. One of the bystanders reckons he's some kind of cat shifter. We haven't managed to get an ID, but I wondered if it might be your brother?"

My chest constricted. *No.*

It couldn't be.

I'd come so close to losing my father and younger siblings less than two weeks ago. Far too close. Close enough that I'd glimpsed the black, empty ocean of despair their absence would plunge me into. And that glimpse had damn near broken me.

This couldn't be happening. Not again. My heart felt like it'd sprouted a set of wings and was attempting clumsy, panicked flight around my rib cage.

I mumbled something even I didn't catch and hung up on dispatch so I could call home. "Dad, are Blake and Archer with you?"

"Sure, darling. What's up?"

"Are you *sure* they're with you?"

Miles was by no means a lax parent. As a vampire, he was particularly hard to get things past. But Blake might manage it. Especially if his brother Archer was covering for him.

And as much as I hated to even entertain the thought, Blake *was* a sensitive kid—smart and observant and deep-thinking. The world could be unkind to those who saw and felt too much. And yes, okay, he did have a peculiar fascination with end-of-life funerary rites. But I'd thought that was just him doing him—not a cry for help.

No.

Only two weeks ago, my younger brother had been fighting to live. I refused to believe that had changed.

"Both definitely here," Dad confirmed. "Now, are you going to tell me why you sound like you've been drained of several pints of blood?"

"Later. But thanks."

I hung up, feeling horrible for the relief that washed

over me. Whoever was up on that cell tower was *someone's* kid. Someone's brother or best friend.

I had to stop him from jumping.

How I was going to do that, I had no idea. But it had to mean *something* that he'd asked for me, right?

Something, yes. But what? Something good or something bad? My brain spun like the wheels of a mired car, failing to land on an answer.

The cell tower came into view.

It was one of those towers disguised as a palm tree, and my scrambling mind helpfully put two and two together.

A *cat* stuck up a *tree*. Sort of.

I tried to rub my face and clunked my helmet instead. *Focus, Lyra.*

"Can you get me close enough to shout but not so close as to scare him?"

Aurelis scoffed. "If you have to ask after all these months of seeing my majesty up close, I've actually managed to *under*estimate your dimwittedness."

I rolled my eyes. "I meant it as a request, not questioning your ability."

"Then you should've used proper syntax."

I had just enough time to wonder *why* I'd missed this and whether it was a sign something was wrong with me—because I absolutely had—before Aurelis brought me in close to the giant artificial palm fronds and the small dark-haired boy perched precariously in their midst.

I shoved up my helmet's visor so he could see my face while Aurelis's wings worked to subjugate gravity.

"Hey," I called. "I'm Officer Lyra Ridley. My dragon partner's going to drop me up on the tower so we can talk like you wanted, okay?"

I had to introduce myself because, despite his superficial resemblance to Blake, I was almost certain I'd never seen him before. And I didn't want my sudden arrival on the tower to startle him into jumping.

He nodded, his gaze spending more time on Aurelis than me. She dropped away to gain speed and momentum before climbing upward again. Then executed a perfect barrel roll and used a splash of her magic to deposit me on the postage-stamp-sized platform near the center of the tower.

I dropped into a crouch, lowering my center of gravity to combat my sudden vertigo.

I could've done without the barrel roll.

The rectangular steel mesh grating meant there was more air than metal beneath my feet, but I pressed my fingers into the lines of steel and found it reassuringly solid. The boy was only five yards away. Five yards away across a treacherously narrow beam. But close.

I made the mistake of looking down. Past the spiky green plastic-and-fiberglass palm fronds.

A small crowd had gathered around the base of the barbed and chain-linked fence that was supposed to keep things like this from happening.

They were very far away.

11

And while generally I wasn't bad with heights, I was all too aware that a cat's ability to land on their feet wouldn't help a whit in this situation.

I tapped my comm to make sure Aurelis could hear everything that was going on. "Um, Aurelis? Stay close enough for a rescue attempt in case he jumps, okay?"

Or if I slip and fall trying to get to him, I thought, as I eyed the length of steel leading to the antenna he was sitting beside. It had no platform grating, no hand-holds, nor anything else remotely useful for hanging onto. And I'd have to duck under a palm frond along the way.

I removed my helmet and, for want of a better place to put it, clipped the heavy clunky thing onto my duty belt. Then stood up and forced my tense jaw into a friendly smile. "Hi there. You wanted to talk to me?"

The kid glanced at me, then down at the ground far below.

Don't even think about it, I mentally growled at him. But I kept the smile pinned to my face and stepped out onto the steel beam.

Easy, right? If I'd been walking along a similar width beam resting on the ground, I'd have no doubt of making it across without a misstep.

It was another hot cloudless day, and I was grateful for the still conditions even as I longed for a breeze to cool the sweat pricking my skin.

The kid didn't react, so I kept going. Step by careful step.

He was slight enough that I could probably over-power him if I had to. *If* I could get within reach.

But I hoped I'd be able to convince him there were better alternatives to snuffing out his life when it had barely begun.

"What's your name?" I tried again while I edged closer. And then when he didn't respond, "Do you go to school with my brothers, Blake and Archer? They're shifters like you."

That got his attention. He looked at me sharply, then sniffed the air, as if trying to figure out why *I* wasn't a shifter.

My heart ached at that close-up view. His age and coloring were so similar to Blake's, with a mop of thick, dark hair he was often too distracted to brush and the same bright green-gold eyes shared by many large cats. But this boy's brow was scrunched in distress instead of concentration, and he was hunched in on himself like he was going to be sick. An unsettling posture in someone so young.

"Whatever's wrong, we can talk about it, and I'll do everything I can to help," I promised. "I won't judge."

But he didn't say a word. Even though he must have talked to someone earlier to ask for me.

Why had he asked for me?

I returned to the topic he'd sort of reacted to. "Do you have any brothers or sisters?"

He shrugged, and I held my breath, waiting.

"Just a little sister."

"Oh. Sorry."

That dragged his attention back to me. "What do you mean?"

"Well"—I silently apologized to Sage—"sometimes little sisters can be kind of annoying…"

He snorted. But I was pretty sure it was an agreeable rather than scoffing sound.

All the while as I talked, I inched closer. Keeping my movements slow and gentle.

Either he didn't notice or he didn't care. Or he wanted me closer.

Maybe he didn't really want to jump.

Maybe this was about something else. Why else would he ask for a cop? Was he in trouble? Were his parents in trouble? Or—despite the hot sun, a chill brushed over me—had I arrested one of his parents?

But the fear and apprehension on his face were plain to see, and I didn't sense a shred of animosity.

I changed tack. "Nice view from up here." Perhaps starting with a less personal topic would help.

He didn't roll his eyes or turn away from me, so I kept going. "Do you like climbing? My brother Blake's animal form is a black jaguar, and he loves climbing trees."

He shrugged again and shifted his gaze outward. "Sometimes."

It was only one word, but at least he was talking. I had to keep him going. Keep snagging his interest. His

14

gaze was taking in that view I'd just admired, but I noticed it linger on Aurelis.

"Well, you must be a good climber," I concluded. "Because this is way too high for me."

"But you were flying on a dragon!"

Gotcha.

"True, but that's different." I chewed my lip, pretending to think... "Would *you* like to fly on a dragon? I could ask if she'd let you?"

Aurelis was going to kill me.

For a moment, his face lit up like it was Christmas. But the delight fell away with a speed that made my stomach drop with it.

"Nah."

He stared down at the ground again. But not before I caught the pain and fear and confusion he was doing his best to hide.

Geez, he was so young. Too young to contemplate something so permanent, so final as this. What had happened to him? Was he being bullied like my poor little sister? Abused? Misunderstood? Or maybe an unmanaged mental illness was pushing him toward despair? I hoped I could convince him to tell me. Trust me. Talk with me. And then I hoped like hell I could actually help.

But before any of that, I needed to get into a position where I could grab him if the talking stuff didn't pan out.

Moving carefully, I lowered myself on the steel

framing beside him, trying to figure out how I could wedge myself in as securely as possible.

He glanced up while I was still getting into position, bright green-gold eyes landing on mine before flicking away again.

That was when he shoved me.

CHAPTER TWO

He was only small, but he had shifter strength and speed, and I was off balance.

I fell.

Saw his face change to a strange mix of satisfaction and horror as he witnessed the effect of that shove...

Heard myself scream.

A fake palm frond smacked into my back, and I snatched at it. Missed. Caught the next one. But my own weight and momentum yanked it away from me, the plastic and fiberglass shredding the skin from my fingers as they slipped down its length. Unable to halt my descent.

And then there were no more palm fronds. Nothing but air between me and that barbed wire fence and the ground below.

I was going to die.

The wind roared in my ears. Tearing at my hair, my skin, my clothes, but doing nothing to save me.

Belatedly, I remembered my new chain magic. The one I'd been trying so hard not to use. But I'd already fallen too far.

I squeezed my eyes shut.

The force of the wind intensified until it felt almost solid beneath me.

And then I crashed into something with teeth-rattling force. Teeth rattling, but not bone shattering.

Aurelis.

"Wow, that must be a new record even for you," she commented lightly. "From requested companion to so-annoying-I'm-going-to-kill-you in under two minutes. What on earth did you say to him?"

I clung to her familiar sun-warmed scales, unable to summon a response. Unable to sit up. Unable to stop the ragged breathing noises coming out of my throat.

And unable to understand what the frick just happened. Why would this kid try to kill me? And how had I read him so wrong?

Aurelis growled, the rumbling vibration of the sound tangible through our contact. I lifted my head.

The kid in question—the one I'd been trying so hard to rescue—was scampering down the rungs of the tower. As agile as, well, a *cat*.

My jaw moved, but I couldn't get any words out. I was still fighting to get my breathing under control.

I watched him reach the ground safely and felt a jumble of hot anger and sweet relief.

Aurelis descended on him with a rippling snarl that definitely didn't come from her magitech translator.

The kid shrank back, disappearing into a ball of fur I identified as a golden jaguar. Which explained his climbing ability, I supposed. His animal form was still a juvenile and ridiculously cute. He scrambled, trying to run. But Aurelis was already upon him, her front talons blocking his escape.

He flattened himself to the ground, ears and tail dropping in submission to Aurelis's superior threat.

My throat hurt. Probably from the screaming. But worried that my dragon partner might be as mad as she sounded, I sucked some moisture back into my mouth.

"Aurelis, I didn't know you cared."

She snaked her head around to eyeball me. "If anyone's going to kill you for being annoying, it's me."

I gave her neck a quick hug, then slid unsteadily to the ground. "Since I'm beginning to lose track of how many times you've saved my life, that seems fair."

She huffed, but I thought I detected a pleased note to it, then returned her attention to my would-be murderer.

The kid was still in jaguar form. I glared at the adorable fuzzball with his oversized ears and heart-melting Disney eyes, retrieved his torn clothes from the ground, and shooed away the gawking bystanders. "Change," I ordered. "We need to talk."

He hesitated, although his body language was still submissive.

Aurelis growled to back me up.

He shifted. And I dropped the clothes into his lap. He studiously avoided looking at me.

"What's your name?" I demanded, my anger winning out now that we were all safely on the ground.

"Dylan."

"Dylan," I repeated. "Care to explain why, for crying out loud, you just tried to kill me?"

His posture changed, his spine stiffening and chest inflating to make himself bigger. And if he'd still had a tail, it doubtless would've been swishing.

His eyes had gone sort of blank, but they met mine and held them.

"The devil made me do it," he said.

CHAPTER THREE

I snorted. But his gaze was steady and his expression eerily serene. The effect was creepy even though I knew he must be lying.

"The *devil* made you do it? Come on, kid. At least try to be original."

His skin rippled with a glimmer of tawny fur like he was trying to shake off a fly. "It's true. He made me."

I'd made some enemies in my short career. But I was pretty sure none of them had a direct line to the devil.

At least I hoped not.

Aurelis did another one of her threatening growls, but while he hunched back in on himself and looked away, he just said, "Can I see my mom now?"

"Yes. I'd quite like to speak to her myself." I glanced at the cell tower. "I don't suppose you have her phone number, do you?"

We'd just loaded Dylan into a patrol car and

arranged for his mother to meet him at the station when dispatch called again.

"Mr. Vargas's neighbor just reported he's on the move. Apparently drove his tank straight through their shared fence and over her husband's BMW."

What on earth? Was this whole tank thing some sort of bizarre neighborly dispute?

Ugh. The paperwork on this was going to be a nightmare.

"And um, did this neighbor happen to say what Mr. Vargas did after that?"

"Drove down the wrong side of the street and over a few extra parked vehicles along the way. He's now on Flamingo Road, heading toward the Strip. We've sent patrols, but we might need Aurelis's special skill set for this one."

I was already clambering up her scales.

"On our way."

"Good. We'll keep you apprised."

Aurelis exploded into flight.

I fumbled to put on my helmet.

It turned out a tank could move pretty fast on a good-quality road. By the time we arrived, it was zipping along at about forty-five miles per hour down the three-lane highway. Three patrol cars were hemming Vargas in, sirens blaring. But since they had no hope of forcing him off the road or forming a blockade he couldn't just drive over, all they were really managing to do was clear the traffic ahead of him like a handy police escort.

It was saving civilian lives, but it was also getting Mr. Vargas closer to his end goal faster.

Whatever his end goal was…

The lead patrol car backed off, and one of the officers threw up a wall of ice. The tank plowed straight through it. The police vehicles had to slow and swerve through the hole it made.

I took some comfort in the fact Vargas wasn't using the guns so far. Then again, perhaps without a crew, he couldn't shoot and drive at the same time.

Or perhaps he just hadn't met a threat worth shooting at yet.

I skimmed through the copy of the permit we'd been given when we'd first been assigned the job and dialed his phone number.

It rang six times before—to my surprise—he picked up.

"Mr. Vargas, what on earth are you doing?"

"I'm afraid I can't tell you that."

"What's your target?"

"I can't tell you that either."

"What's your plan here? Surely you know this can't end well for you."

"Yes," he agreed heavily.

I waited, but he didn't supply the reason he was doing it anyway.

I tried again. "You haven't killed anyone yet. If you pull over now, I'll tell the DA to go easy on you."

"I can't."

Those last words came out in a strangled whisper.

"Then why did you answer the phone? I think there's a part of you that doesn't want to do this. Maybe a big part..."

The call disconnected, and I cursed.

Below, someone in the patrol cars laid a sheet of ice over the road this time. The tank slid when it hit the frozen layer, but it was going straight enough that it just regained traction on the other side.

"Do you think you can get us in close and land on top of the tank?" I asked Aurelis. She was practically bulletproof, and he hadn't shot anyone so far. "Maybe we can take out the externally mounted turret guns."

If we could minimize his firepower, we could at least minimize the havoc he could wreak.

Aurelis twitched irritably. "What did I tell you about questioning my abilities?"

But she plunged into a dive that left my stomach behind. The tank seemed both smaller and larger than I remembered as she prepared to come down on top of the speeding platform.

She matched the vehicle's speed and landed, talons scraping against the metal. "Destroy anything that looks like it could be a sensor or camera," she advised. "Without those, he won't be able to see a thing."

I wasn't sure I wanted to force Vargas to drive blind with me clinging to the top, but I slid down from Aurelis's neck and started looking for anything that might fit that description. *After* I found a firm hand-hold, that is.

The tank wasn't as fast as a dragon, but the wind whipped my uniform around my body all the same, and the blaring sirens and flashing lights were no more soothing than the asphalt streaking past below.

I kept my helmet on.

Dispatch chimed in my ear again. "All units pursuing the tank on Flamingo Road, we have a chopper and an anti-tank gun on standby."

On standby because a gun that could blow up a tank was going to do serious damage to more than just the target. And Mr. Vargas still hadn't killed anyone yet.

A last resort.

I found a camera-looking thing and shot it. Then scanned for my next target.

Aurelis focused on the weapons.

She bent the mounted machine gun out of commission with a single thwack of her powerful tail and turned her attention to the main gun. Its huge barrel was almost as long again as the tank itself. She tried sabotaging *it* with her tail too. Once. Twice. A third time. It dented but didn't bend. She lowered her long neck and breathed a concentrated stream of flame so hot that even sheltered by her body, I felt like I gained an instant case of sunburn. Then she smashed it again.

It bent at a forty-five-degree angle.

"Nice work," I wheezed. Even my lungs felt like they

were lightly charred. "Maybe if you do that to the armored plating over the engine—"

A sudden jolt as the tank swung onto a new, smaller road almost sent me flying without the aid of my dragon partner. What would happen if Vargas started *trying* to fling me off?

But even as I clawed my way back into position, knuckles white against the pocket of metal I was using as a handhold and my friction-burned fingers whining in protest, my brain registered what I'd seen. The hatch on top of the turret had jumped up an inch before thumping back into place. Had Vargas not bothered to lock it down?

It didn't make sense. Why go on an illegal rampage in a near-impenetrable armored vehicle without securing yourself inside?

Though I suppose he could've been planning a rapid getaway and might be forgiven for not anticipating dragon-borne gatecrashers.

More importantly, what was his end goal? His target?

We'd just turned down a road that ran parallel to the Strip, except one street over. If he'd wanted to head south, there were better routes to take, so I figured we must be getting close. But close to what?

We were now traveling through a predominantly commercial district, but one not nearly as popular or shiny-glamorous as the bustling, casino-laden tourist attraction. The only worthwhile thing on this road from my perspective was the dingy little restaurant that made the best Vietnamese takeout in the city. I was perpetually grateful it *wasn't* on the Strip or else its prices would've tripled.

But I couldn't think of anything here worth blowing up.

Unless it was personal. Did Vargas have a cheating partner who lived or worked on this street? Dispatch hadn't provided that information. Though no doubt an officer somewhere was trying to dig into his history and possible motives now. And anyway, we'd disabled his guns, so...

Unless he didn't realize they were disabled?

I supposed it would only be polite to tell him.

"Hang on," I yelled to Aurelis. "I'm going in."

The tank had slowed a little in concession to the smaller, less well-maintained road, but the vibration and shaking had gotten worse. Maybe Vargas should've had the suspension looked at while it was here for a "wash." Did tanks have suspension?

I pulled myself over to the hatch and heaved on the handle. It opened—almost sending me flying a second time—but I flattened myself against the top of the turret and peered cautiously inside.

I couldn't see a freaking thing.

Well, I could see lots of things I didn't understand, but the interior was too cramped and the driver's station too far forward for me to spy from the narrow access well of the turret.

I would have to go in blind.

Even so, I took off my helmet so I'd at least have better peripheral vision. Then, hoping it wasn't a trap, I checked my weapons, braced myself on the provided handholds, and lowered myself down the access well.

The interior didn't get any less cramped once you were inside. But I could see Vargas now. Or at least I could see a slice of him through the unfamiliar jungle of metal parts, seats, storage, and instruments.

He glanced back, tension written all over his face.

I threw myself behind an alcove thing to make myself a harder target.

But he didn't move from the controls. Or use them to swerve the tank to unbalance me.

Why not?

"It's over, Mr. Vargas." I had to shout to make myself heard over the noise of the engine and wailing sirens that seemed to ricochet around the bare metal interior like stones in a tin can.

"We've disabled your weapons, so you might as well stop this thing before anyone gets hurt."

But he didn't stop. In fact, he didn't react at all.

My view of him was too limited to see whether he had a handgun or any other weapons on his person. I *could* see that I hadn't managed to disable all the sensors because a screen showed a low view of the same familiar street.

We were only a hundred yards from the Vietnamese

place. Maybe I'd grab a banh mi for lunch when I was done here.

Still shielding the bulk of my body behind the alcove, I raised my Taser until I had a line of sight. "Stop the vehicle. Now. Or I'll shoot!"

Once again, he failed to react.

Unease crept through my gut. What was the play here? What was so important he was ignoring a potential threat to his life? He couldn't *know* I was aiming a Taser instead of a gun—not when he hadn't bothered to look back.

I spent a few precious seconds trying to make sense of the levers and controls that lacked anything like the steering wheel, foot pedals, and gears of a manually driven car. I didn't want to take Vargas down only to crash the tank myself.

Of course, I couldn't learn how to brake from observation if he didn't do it first.

Instead of braking, Vargas fiddled with the controls, and the tank swerved, heading straight for a building. Son of a bitch. My favorite restaurant!

Still not knowing if I could stop the blasted thing, still not knowing whether he had a weapon on him, I lunged.

The Taser hit him between his shoulder blades, but I didn't pause to check the effect. There were people in that restaurant. I yanked his hands away from the controls.

The tank didn't stop, vaulting instead up the curb to the outdoor dining area.

Shit.

People screamed and dove out of the way as I helplessly scanned the array of screens and buttons and levers. Praying I wasn't about to do something incredibly stupid, I wrenched the two-lever joystick thing downward.

Glass and bricks shattered. Metal screeched. Dust clouded the camera screen. But the tank jerked to a halt.

A halt two feet *inside* the restaurant. But at least it stopped.

The question was, how many had it hurt in the process?

I spun on Vargas and cuffed him as the last of the Taser charge fizzled out. Then changed out my Taser cartridge and leveled it at him again. "It's over, Mr. Vargas," I repeated a little unsteadily. "Don't try anything."

He didn't resist. Didn't struggle. Even though he'd have a decent chance of gaining the upper hand in the cramped confines with his military background, extra weight, and familiarity with the space. He didn't do anything but look resigned and maybe even faintly relieved.

What was with people today? The kid I'd tried to save from himself tried to kill me, and the guy who'd nearly murdered a bunch of innocents sat there and cooperated as meek as a lamb.

Still, I kept my Taser trained on him.

"You're under arrest for reckless endangerment, evading law enforcement, willful destruction of private and public property, assault with a deadly weapon, attempted murder, driving an unauthorized vehicle, and... Well, you get the drift. But I'm sure they'll go through all the charges with you at the station. Once they've finished tallying them up."

He was shaking his head by the time I was done. "It's not my fault, I swear."

Aurelis snorted through our shared comm. And I suddenly wanted to get out of this blind metal contraption more than anything. Had everyone gotten out of the way in time? Even my partner might've been injured if she'd tried to get between the tank and the building.

"Save it," I snapped. "Do you know how many people you almost murdered? Get up."

He obeyed, extricating himself awkwardly from the congested driving nook and moving toward the access well with his hands cuffed behind his back.

Aurelis yanked him out as soon as his head cleared the open hatch, and I levered myself out after him, relieved she appeared unscathed.

The same could not be said for the building. Half a dozen uniformed officers were tending to the shaken customers and staff. At least five people were wounded, probably from the explosion of glass and brick.

"Really," Vargas insisted as Aurelis planted him none too gently on the sidewalk. "It's not my fault."

31

I wasn't listening, too busy checking the vicinity for other unmoving victims. Thank goodness it was too early in the day for the modest little restaurant to be busy yet.

"The devil made me do it."

That got my attention.

Aurelis's eyes met mine.

What the hell? Was there a new drug on the streets I hadn't heard about?

I patted Vargas down, surprised when I didn't find a gun on him, considering the nature of his business.

"I left them at home," he told me. "I didn't want to do this. Why would I want to do this? Look at my poor tank. It will cost a fortune to fix the damage."

He was right. None of this made sense. Nobody drove an armored tank through a restaurant because they'd forgotten the complimentary spring rolls or something.

Two hours into my first day back at work and my head was starting to ache.

I scanned the area again to reassure myself that at least no one was grievously injured.

Which was when someone walked past in a bright red mascot-style devil costume, complete with an oversized stuffed head.

CHAPTER FOUR

I blinked. Once. Twice.

Nobody would choose to walk around in a heavily padded full-body costume in the heat of Las Vegas. It would be like an oven in there. And after the day I'd had so far, it was too weird, too specific, and too perfectly timed to be a coincidence.

"Aurelis, can you keep an eye on Vargas? I want to follow that devil guy."

"Why do you get the fun job?"

"Because it's hard to be inconspicuous when you're a majestic one-of-a-kind dragon?"

"Oh sure. Because head-to-toe khaki is *so* much better. I'm not letting you go alone. Cuff him to the tank or something."

I hesitated, but there were plenty of officers milling around and probably more coming, so I unearthed a second pair of handcuffs and did as she suggested. Then jogged after the devil. He or she had continued in the direction of the Strip, walking neither fast nor slow, at just the right pace to not draw attention.

An entirely futile effort given the outfit.

Aurelis took to the skies where she'd be less visible, and I followed at a distance. As she'd pointed out, my uniform wasn't exactly inconspicuous either.

We reached the Strip where it was easier to hide myself among the other pedestrians, but easier too for even a bright red pitchfork-wielding cartoon character to pull a disappearing act. I sped up so I wouldn't lose him.

The devil turned in to one of the smaller casinos, and I hung back, uncertain. Oh. Maybe they were just an entertainer. That would make sense. People did crazier things for money than parade around in the stinking heat inside sweltering polyester costumes.

Like choose to be cops, for example.

But still. The timing. The coincidence. It was too weird.

What did I have to lose?

The casino was relatively empty. Most revelers were still sleeping off the night before, which left the hardcore gamblers who hadn't gone to bed yet, a few noisy, wide-eyed tour groups, and the local seniors who liked to finish up their morning coffees with a quick try at the slot machines.

I followed the devil into the unused stairwell beside the elevators. With no crowd to blend with, it was likely they knew I was behind them now. Although I figured the giant stuffed head would do a number on their peripheral vision, and it would likely interfere with their hearing too.

I stayed one staircase behind and wished for a less recognizable outfit.

The figure in fluffy red hiked sixteen flights all the way up to the rooftop. The stairwell was thankfully cool, but I was still starting to perspire by the time we reached the twelfth floor. I could only imagine how uncomfortable it must be inside the sauna suit.

If they were an entertainer, why wouldn't they at least take the stuffed head off? For that matter, why not take the elevator?

Yet at no point did the suspect pause for a breather or turn around to ask me why the heck I was following them. Instead, they pushed open the door to the rooftop nightclub and went through.

I rushed up the last set of stairs, whispering an update to Aurelis, and peered through the square of glass in the door.

This particular nightclub—Aurora—was known for its floating "chandelier" that had been magicked to imitate the northern lights in all their glory. I didn't hang out in nightclubs, but they'd held a special family event during the most recent school holidays, and Blake had dragged us all along. I had to admit the effect was mesmerizing at night. I still had a photo taped to my fridge of the five of us grinning down at the camera with the lights flickering above.

The magicked rectangular sheet of glass that hung over the dance floor was much *less* effective in the middle of this clear and sunny day. Which was probably why no one else was up here.

The cartoon devil had walked over to the far edge of the abandoned rooftop and propped their pitchfork against the glass balustrade. Their huge head was down, and they were fiddling with the front of their suit. I couldn't see well from my vantage in the stairwell.

Then they were holding something else. And it wasn't a plastic pitchfork.

Oh hell no. The devil had a submachine gun.

Horror clamped around my throat like a werewolf's teeth as I imagined the suspect opening fire on the unsuspecting pedestrians below. No gentle seduction of souls here. He would straight-out extinguish them forever—with a mere crook of his finger against the trigger.

I was too far away to stop it.

I gave up on stealth, hissing a plea to Aurelis and shoving open the door. My own gun was drawn, my Taser not an option at this distance or against that outfit. But if I shot first and without warning, I'd be in a world of trouble. And that infernal padded costume hid the contours of the person's body as well as it had hidden the submachine gun, making a clear shot impossible.

I was sprinting across the dance floor, shouting at them to put the gun down even as my brain was pointing out how I should've stayed behind the door. If the devil turned that weapon my way, there was no cover on this rooftop. And my body armor only protected my torso.

But what if there was a good reason the shooter was still wearing that ridiculous suit, oversized head and all, even as they prepared to fire? What if the costume was magicked to be bulletproof?

A submachine gun could spray an awful lot of bullets in the seconds it'd take me to figure that out from the relative safety of the stairwell.

The figure raised the barrel of the gun. It seemed to happen in slow motion. Past the harmless swathe of floor. Past the edge of the rooftop. Past the top of the glass balustrade. And then time slammed back into full throttle as he opened fire on the Strip.

Copper flashed a few yards below as Aurelis attempted to take the brunt of the bullets on her impenetrable scales. Thwarted, the shooter whirled to face me and raised the barrel a second time.

I dove and rolled. But no bullets chewed into the floor around me. Instead, the devil aimed at the floating expanse of glass above and pulled the trigger.

The "chandelier" must have been tempered because it didn't immediately shatter into a million pieces. But the rigging swayed and groaned under the assault, and long, foreboding cracks raced across the length of the glass. A few more seconds of gunfire and the ensuing avalanche of giant broken shards would kill us both.

I was sprawled on the dance floor halfway across the rooftop, halfway through pulling my own trigger, when I remembered my new forbidden magic. I could shoot to kill and possibly misjudge, possibly fail to incapacitate him in time, or—

The chain snapped out from my free hand with satisfying alacrity and yanked the gun from the shooter's grasp.

The barrage of bullets cut off.

And the glowing links of the chain carried the weapon back to me. I snatched the submachine gun out of the air left-handed and let the links dissolve, my own weapon still trained on the shooter. Who knew what other tricks he might have up his bright red sleeve?

Above us, the fractured glass groaned and shifted.

The devil didn't move.

"Raise your hands. And take that damn costume head off!"

Aurelis joined me on the rooftop, neatly tucking her wings at the last possible second to fit through the gap between the balustrade, the swaying damaged glass ceiling, and the rigging cables thankfully still holding it aloft.

She glared at the shooter, smoke curling upward from her terrifying maw. She *really* disliked having to buff out bullet scratches from her scales. Yet she'd done as I'd requested anyway.

I trusted she wasn't hurt but didn't dare split my concentration to ask about the pedestrians.

The devil slowly lifted his now empty hands and pulled off the giant grinning head.

My jaw dropped. The face underneath was familiar. Flushed and sweating but familiar.

"Stewie?"

Stewie was my sometimes homeless, frequently sober, and always paranoid criminal informant. His heightened distrust combined with his honorable heart and magically augmented hearing made him a useful if tricky CI I found impossible not to like. And up until sixty seconds ago when he'd tried to murder me and countless others, I'd have said he was as earnest and loyal as his little dog Zeus.

Now, he stared at the floor.

There was no way *he* hadn't heard me following him all the way up here. So if his intent had been to kill, why not take me down first so he could get on with it in peace?

"Sorry, boss."

"What on earth is going on here? Why are you running around playing dress-up with a submachine gun?"

And trying to murder people.

Could he be in the middle of one of his more extreme episodes and on so many drugs they'd shoved him past lines he'd never normally cross?

Stewie raised his chin, a sudden blankness sweeping across his features.

"Don't say it," Aurelis warned.

My CI spoke in a flat, inflectionless voice. "The devil made me do it."

Aurelis groaned.

Stewie had said the same thing as everyone else, but his eyes blinked rapidly—like they were trying to tell me something different.

"What do you mean? Are you being threatened? Is someone watching us?" The question brought the surveillance cameras into focus, and I winced at my now not-so-secret new magic. But that wasn't the most pressing problem at present. "Where's Zeus?"

My informant friend's raised hands shook, and part of me really wanted to let him lower them, but I couldn't. The whole city had gone bonkers today.

I lowered my voice to the barest whisper so that no audio surveillance should be able to pick up on it. So that only my CI could hear. "Stewie, where's Zeus? Is he okay?"

His face contorted in some internal struggle, and my heart stuttered. But when he spoke again after one of the longer pauses of my life, he said, "Don't worry about us, boss. It's you he wants."

The hair pricked on the back of my neck. Then icy fingers traced the curve of my spine as I put the details together in a new light.

The boy on the tower who'd asked for me. Who'd just so happened to look like my brother. The tank on a senseless rampage through the city—apparently on a mission to put my favorite takeout place out of business.

Stewie walking past in a flashy devil's costume at just the right moment to catch my eye. Leading to this scene at the one nightclub in the city I had some recent association with.

This was personal.

And yet there was something else. Something almost... playful about the events. The "cat" up a "tree." The wild thrill ride of an armored tank loose in a city— which could've been wielded far more effectively if the goal was death or destruction or even to wound me personally. The absurdity of a cartoon-style devil, a freaking submachine gun, and the untargeted, slapdash dealing of death.

This was a *game* to the person responsible.

A test.

Only a warm-up for what was to come.

"Who, Stewie? Who's behind this?"

My CI shuddered.

"The devil," he said.

CHAPTER FIVE

I was right. The paperwork was a nightmare.

The questioning of the various perps was worse.

A detective trained in interview techniques spoke to Dylan and his mother as well as Vargas while Aurelis and I watched on. But I spoke to Stewie since I was the only one he might trust.

Everyone more or less cooperated—until they were asked anything about who had forced them to carry out their strange tasks or how they'd been coerced into acting.

Even so, we'd managed to glean some information from what they *didn't* say…

Poor Stewie, who was so at ease and cheerful on the streets, was visibly distressed in the precinct. Even after he'd taken off the devil costume to reveal the overlarge lavender rain shell jacket he always wore—in spite of Vegas's near-constant sunny weather—he looked nothing like his usual self.

I hated seeing him like that. And I was worried about what would happen to him while we cleared this mess up. Worried what would happen afterward as well. Thanks to Aurelis, no one had been hurt, but attempted murder with a submachine gun was a serious offense, and there was a lot of property damage to be accounted for. Proving he'd acted under duress would lighten his sentence, but jail time was still a real possibility.

And freedom meant everything to Stewie. He valued it above security, above safety, above a guaranteed meal or a comfortable place to sleep.

If he went to prison, I feared he wouldn't survive it.

My fingers clenched in anger at the injustice of the situation.

How had the man—because that was the one detail all the perps, or victims rather, let slip—even snuck up on my CI friend? Between his paranoia and unrivaled hearing, Stewie was well capable of looking after himself. Sometimes I even wondered if he'd had special-ops training somewhere in his mysterious past. But he didn't like to talk about his history, so I'd never pressed.

"Will you tell me where Zeus is? I'd like to check on him for you."

I was asking for two reasons. One, because I really did want to make sure the little dog was okay and was hoping I might be able to sneak him into the precinct to comfort Stewie. Two, because if I wanted to convince

Stewie to do something against his will, Zeus was the obvious leverage point.

We still hadn't managed to uncover the mechanism the puppet master was using to force our three individuals to act. But I had a discomforting suspicion it wasn't leverage at all.

If Zeus was safe, it would help validate that hunch. Unwelcome as that validation might be.

Stewie studied my face for a long time before answering. "Hold my hand."

I hesitated. I'd removed his cuffs earlier, trying to lessen the panic-inducing pressure of being confined. But I'd been careful to keep my distance since then. Just in case. He might be a good thirty years my senior, his dark blond hair salted white now, and no more than my match in height, but he was built with a compact sturdiness I didn't underestimate.

I understood what he was really asking. He knew about my magic. That I could borrow powers from others. I'd borrowed his on more than one occasion. He even knew I could apparently *steal* it forever if I was willing to kill the original owner for it. But right now he was asking me to draw on his magic so he could tell me something the recorders wouldn't pick up.

He'd noticed my hesitation.

The hurt on his round, honest face clinched it for me.

Trust was difficult for Stewie, and yet he'd repeatedly

placed his trust in me. The least I could do was extend the same faith.

I reached for his callused palm and *tugged*.

A maelstrom of sound rushed in, drowning out my other senses. The sharp boom of a door closing. Conversations in neighboring rooms that felt like they were being spoken in overloud voices directly into my ear canals. The abrasive scratch of pen on paper. Someone making coffee in the break room. Someone *slurping* coffee in the break room. The distracting clicking and clacking and ticking of countless keyboards, computer mice, and clocks.

I squeezed my eyes shut and focused on reining it in. Focused on this room only. On the man sitting across from me, his roughened palm in mine. Then I looked up and gave him a nod.

He covered his mouth with his other hand to prevent lip reading. And then he gave me a location.

Of course I couldn't write it down. Couldn't breach his trust like that. So I committed it to memory.

"Thank you. I'll check on him as soon as I can."

I let go and attempted a reassuring smile. But I suspected Stewie was too perceptive to be reassured.

He didn't become noticeably less tense.

I was doing my job as I usually would, acting like this morning was nothing out of the ordinary, like I had everything under control, like the whole thing was no more than a stupid stunt. But the truth was, I was more than a little creeped out.

It wasn't just the "playful" nature or the devil references or even the idea that whoever was behind this was focused on me. It was the growing realization that this manipulator—whoever he was—had done his research. An unsettling level of research. He knew what my little brother looked like. He knew my favorite takeout place. He even knew about my relationship with Stewie. Which was nuts, because we rarely had any contact with each other, and our agreement wasn't on any official records by Stewie's insistence.

Worse, the creep knew I'd visited the nightclub Aurora. Which implied he'd either been stalking me for over a month unnoticed—or he'd been inside my apartment.

How closely had he been watching me? And for how long?

If he knew all those things—and this morning's events had proven he was more than capable of using the things I cared about against me with no regard for who might get hurt along the way—I was terrified of how things would escalate once he *stopped* playing around.

Before Stewie could comment on whatever he'd read in my expression, Captain Gadson opened the door. In contrast to my frazzled state, the captain's uniform was neatly pressed and immaculate, his steel-gray buzz cut tidy, and his bearing quietly authoritative.

"See me in my office, Ridley."

"Yes, sir."

A ghost of a smile deepened the lines on Stewie's weathered face. "The boss's boss, eh?"

I summoned a smile to offer in return, one tinged with genuine amusement this time. "That's right. Excuse me for a bit."

I followed Gadson into his office.

The last time I'd been in here, he'd suspended me for borrowing a bystander's magic without permission to save a little girl's life. A whiny jerk of a bystander who'd wanted to see me punished. The suspension had been to stop the jerk from pressing charges and maintain positive public relations.

That had been before a cult had taken Las Vegas hostage and threatened the lives of every supernatural caught in its trap. Before I'd gone on an unsanctioned mission to save my city. Before my magic had proven far more useful than I'd given it credit for—and then changed my understanding of it forever.

My concerns had been so much smaller then.

"Take a seat."

I sat. And tried not to shift under Gadson's appraisal. He was a good boss in an endlessly high-pressure environment stuck juggling the competing needs of keeping the higher-ups, the public, and his large, diverse force of interspecies personnel happy. He did a damn fine job of it given the circumstances, and I respected him for that.

I also tried not to add to his problems if I could help it.

Tried but often failed.

The captain steepled his fingers on the well-ordered desk. "I know it's not a sure thing yet, but I believe we can take a reasonable guess at who's behind this morning's events."

All the air leaked out of me.

I *had* been pretty sure, but I'd been hoping we'd follow the path down the rabbit hole and find another explanation. Knowing that Captain Gadson had seen the same threads I had and drawn the same probable conclusion stole my hope for a less dangerous adversary.

Colton Metcalf.

The man with the most powerful mind-control magic in modern history. The man who'd taken over his entire hometown for years without anyone noticing —until he'd gotten bored and moved on to more ambitious projects. He'd lived in the lap of luxury, founded his own power-hungry cult to worship him, and experimented with expanding his power even further by developing horrifying mind-control magitech products with the aid of experts he'd forced to serve him.

It was the malfunctioning of one of those products that'd led to him eventually being caught and locked away in the maximum-security blackout prison here in Vegas. But his apprehension cost the lives of seventeen officers and four bystanders, most of whom had either been killed by someone on their own side or compelled to blow their own brains out.

The psychopath who'd escaped two weeks ago when his cult had taken the city hostage.

The scheme I'd taken a lead role in bringing to an unsuccessful end.

I'd looked into Metcalf more thoroughly since then. Since the day he'd been inside my family home, grinning at me through the camera lens, thanking me for unwittingly helping him escape, and threatening the lives of my father and youngest siblings.

Dad had taught us that the assignation of magic gifts to each human was like a lottery system. That it hadn't been possible to set limits or base the strength of a power on merit or logic rather than pure chance. *Because magic is a force of nature like any other. It is not the tool that tills the field, lifeless unless a farmer picks it up. It is the fiery sun our world revolves around, the rain and wind and ice that throw themselves upon the earth. Forces the farmer can use and harness to some degree, but never tame or control.*

When it came to Metcalf, magic had made a colossal mistake.

At thirteen years of age, a few weeks after he'd come into his full power, he'd forced his best friend to eat his own finger. For fun.

Even more unsettling was the fact this friend still followed Metcalf everywhere with unwavering loyalty until his parents moved him and his remaining fingers across the country.

Metcalf had been showing psychopathic traits even

before the magic revolution had hit at the age of six. A lifetime of convincing anyone to give him anything he wanted had done nothing to curb those tendencies. Unconstrained by the normal pressures that molded the average person into acting within the bounds of cultural acceptability—that of empathy, the ability to feel shame, fear of punishment, and the desire to please or belong—he was narcissistic, easily bored, and driven solely by self-gratification.

Metcalf was intelligent, but his plans, while methodical, were driven by perverse self-indulgence rather than logic. And he pursued his goals without any fear or feeling to hold him in check.

It made him volatile.

And now he was fixated on me.

Gadson was watching my face carefully. "I'd like you to consider going into police protection. A safe house. Until Metcalf is either apprehended or grows bored with his current game and moves on to a fresh obsession."

My stomach turned over.

The thing was, with Metcalf's powers of mind control, *nowhere* would be safe. All he needed was to talk to one person who knew where I was, and they'd tell him everything. And the idea of being cooped up in a safe house unable to contact anyone from the outside world until that day came made my skin crawl.

I supposed I could go on the run and tell no one about my plans or location, but then I'd be utterly without aid or backup too. And how long would it take for the manhunt to be over? How long would I be forced to put my life on hold in an attempt to protect it?

A possibly futile attempt at that.

I didn't know what the answer was. But I knew it was a lot longer than if I stuck around and allowed them to use me as bait.

No. So long as my family was safe, I'd prefer to stand and fight with law enforcement to back me up. At least this way I might have a hope of seeing Metcalf coming.

Besides, we didn't know whether he could manipulate dragons. Maybe Aurelis would be able to resist his compulsions, in which case she'd be a good person to stay close to.

Not to mention we might be wrong about Metcalf being behind it at all. The fastest way to find out was to stick around and see what the mysterious game player did next.

But if I was going to do that, I had to get my family out of here. Out of the game player's reach. So he couldn't use them against me.

And I could think of only one place they'd be safe.

"Thank you, sir. But I'd prefer to join the team tasked with hunting Metcalf down."

CHAPTER SIX

Gadson accepted my decision without trying to talk me out of it. Maybe he was even relieved. The higher-ups and the press had to be breathing down his neck every day Metcalf remained at large.

"Very well. Use the rest of the day to finish up your paperwork and get your affairs in order. I'll set up an introduction with the task force first thing tomorrow morning."

"Yes, sir. Would it be all right if I ask Aurelis to join the team as well?"

He sighed. "Go ahead."

"Thank you, sir. I know how much you value having a dragon on call within the Rapid Response unit."

"Yes, well, I like having all my officers alive too." I felt touched until he added, "And she and Perez *both* came to me complaining about having to work with each other last week."

I didn't know whether to snicker or wince in sympathy.

He flattened his palms on the desk and gave me a hard stare. "But I want both of you to be very clear on one point. If your decision is to join this task force, you *will* follow orders."

Now I did wince, remembering what happened the last time I'd worked with a task force.

Remembering too that I was already undermining my captain's authority by failing to tell him about the changes in my magic. I still hadn't worked out how I was going to explain the events on the rooftop without mentioning the chain. But maybe that was a moot point. My mind flashed back to the surveillance cameras at Aurora. I should've stuck with plan A and avoided using my new ability.

Except if I had—if I'd shot to kill instead—then removed that grinning devil's head to find Stewie's earnest face underneath...

Bile climbed up my throat. Had that been Metcalf's intention?

Okay, so it was good I'd used the chain magic. Good, but problematic.

I needed to investigate Stewie's theory that my unusual magic was the result of secret artificial experimentation. And that there were certain unscrupulous entities who might be very interested to know I was still alive.

But how? How could you look into something

specifically designed to stay hidden without drawing attention to yourself?

The fact was, even without Stewie's theory, if the press ever caught wind of what had happened... ever learned that a cop could kill people (even in self-defense) and steal their magic, it would be a PR minefield that could end my career.

My ability to temporarily borrow someone's magic —despite not causing any harm whatsoever—had been poorly enough received as it was.

Something akin to panic prickled over my skin. I loved my job. A few days sitting around on paid suspension had driven home how much.

I couldn't lose this.

But now wasn't the time to freak out. I needed every last bit of my focus on dealing with Metcalf.

After that—if I was still alive—I could worry about my disturbing new magic and its effect on my career.

Gadson was watching me, waiting for my agreement.

I unclogged my throat.

"Yes, sir."

After I was dismissed, I found Aurelis and explained the change of direction. "Are you in?"

"Are dragons superior in every way?" she retorted in the tone someone else would ask if the sky was blue.

I grinned, glad that one thing in my life at least remained unchanged.

"Except in the use of handcuffs," I pointed out just to needle her. "But I'll take that as a yes."

"I suppose you *are* better at getting yourself into hot messes too," she mused, and my grin dimmed a little.

I plowed on before she could feel too pleased with herself. "I need to prepare a few things before we get our new orders. Want to come?"

"Are you asking for a partner or transportation?"

"A partner. So long as you're happy to stick to my pace."

She eyeballed me unfavorably, but when I left the precinct, she came along.

"So. Care to explain how you can suddenly conjure a chain from thin air whenever you feel like it?"

I froze midstep. Crap, she *had* seen that. I hadn't been sure…

She kept walking. "I covered your ass by the way. I hacked into the nightclub's servers and corrupted the surveillance footage. Because I assumed anything you're cagey enough about to hide from your *partner* is something you don't want to share with our colleagues and the press."

Guilt and gratitude and relief and regret swamped me all at once.

Aurelis snaked her head down and back at me. I hurried to catch up.

"Was my assumption correct?"

The gaze she leveled my way implied it had better be.

"Y-yes. Thank you. But—"

"If you dare give me another lecture on moral duty right now, I will stomp you flat like the rat you are."

I shut my mouth.

"It'll just be one more thing chalked up to Metcalf's very long, long list of crimes. Now start explaining. Or I might decide to squash you anyway."

Maybe I was feeling overly paranoid after the morning's unsettling events, but I shook my head. "Not here. Not in public. But I promise I'll fill you in later."

Her slitted pupils narrowed. "Yes. You will."

We walked on for a few minutes in silence before I remembered what I was supposed to be doing and pulled out my phone.

When Lord Ronan Nightwing had told me that Faerie owed me a debt and if I ever needed help he'd try to repay it, I hadn't expected to call it in so fast.

I hadn't expected to call it in at all.

But I couldn't think of a safer place for my family than Faerie.

Despite the threat casting its dark and frankly terrifying shadow over my future, I felt a thrill of excitement that I might get to see Ronan again.

Idiot.

I'd have to ask my next date to hire a pair of black wings and get this infatuation out of my system.

Except I'd had enough of costumes for a while. And I hadn't been on a date in months.

Ronan answered on the third ring.

"Lyra?"

"Did you have a chance to miss me, or should I call back later?" There was an awkward silence as he failed to respond, so I rushed on. "Kidding, of course. Sorry, I've had a crazy morning. Which is why I'm calling actually. Do you have a few minutes?"

"Sure." He paused. "Did you find out you have a long-lost evil twin after all?"

The words I'd been queuing up in explanation stumbled and crashed into each other. Huh? *Ohhh*. The telenovela thing. He was—

"Kidding, of course."

Right. Now *I'd* taken too long to respond.

"Of course, sorry. Took me longer than it should."

Aurelis snorted.

I glared at her.

"Lyra, are you all right?" There was real concern coloring Ronan's voice.

I stopped on the sidewalk a second time and exhaled, long and slow. "Not exactly. Were you serious about being able to call on you for help if I ever needed to?"

"I don't make promises I don't intend to keep." His voice had gone stiff. Offended. Honor was important to Ronan.

I exhaled again, apologized again, and explained what I was asking and why.

"I'll find a way to make it happen," he said.

This time I didn't screw up by asking him if he was sure.

"Thank you."

Aurelis snorted again when I hung up. "Well, that was excruciating to listen to."

I gave her another half-hearted glare. "You know providing you with satisfactory entertainment while we carry out our duties isn't actually part of my job description, right?"

"Oh, it was entertaining. Like a B-grade horror film where the girl is too stupid to live."

I considered whether locking myself up in a safe house *without* Aurelis for company might have been a better option after all.

"I'm so glad you decided to come along."

We reached the location Stewie had given me—one of those narrow utility alleys not intended as a thoroughfare. This one smelled worse than average. I scanned the uninviting laneway of windowless, graffiti-riddled brick walls lined with trash cans and dumpsters and realized my words to Aurelis were true. I was glad to have her beside me.

Metcalf might have anticipated that I'd come here.

I stepped over a stray garbage bag that had been stuffed until it had split and was now spilling its contents onto the asphalt. Then I waded through several more that were thankfully still intact. The dumpsters behind them were full. Or the people around here were lazy.

My dragon partner remained on a relatively clean patch of alley. Given her superior sense of smell, I couldn't blame her.

I set to shifting the two large boxes Stewie had told me about. One for a refrigerator. The other unmarked except for unidentifiable dark stains. Like he'd said, they were huge and stank something fierce, but whatever was in them was light.

I held my breath against the assault, keeping every other sense on high alert.

This could be a trap.

After Metcalf had gotten to him, anything Stewie told me was suspect.

I'd been racking my brain, trying to guess what might come next. Except the possibilities were endless. The ability to turn anyone into a devoted accomplice, unquestioningly obedient even in the most extreme and irrational acts, made anticipating the next move damn near impossible.

But I was *pretty* sure I wasn't about to die. Murdering me next to a dumpster wasn't Metcalf's style. Everything he'd done so far had been grandiose. Flashy. Fun. I figured he thought too highly of himself to stoop to something so humdrum.

But there were plenty of horrible things you could do besides kill someone. Many of them worse than death.

I finished moving the boxes, then pulled back the

sheet of corrugated iron that'd been propped against the wall behind the dumpster.

Zeus was exactly where Stewie had told me he'd be. Waiting patiently beside the army-green rucksack his owner usually carried everywhere.

Safe.

Not abducted for leverage.

Because Metcalf didn't need leverage.

A collapsible water bowl sat beside the scruffy little black dog, still mostly full, and a half-eaten meaty bone assured me he hadn't gone hungry. Even so, he wiggled his tail when he saw me, then wiggled his whole body when I offered him a piece of liver jerky.

"Hey, buddy. Wanna come with me?"

I let him sniff my hand, the one that had held Stewie's, and the wiggling became even more enthusiastic. He was some kind of terrier cross and smarter than some people I knew.

I lifted him up, considered the rucksack too, and decided to leave it. Stewie trusted me more than he trusted most people, but I wasn't sure he'd want me to touch his rucksack. And if I was honest, it smelled a lot worse than Zeus did.

Instead, I replaced the iron sheet, the two malodorous boxes, and waded through the garbage bags back to Aurelis.

The dragon looked decidedly *less* pleased at my approach than Zeus had.

"Did you seriously drag me down here just to make a phone call and collect a dog?"

"What?" I challenged, shifting Zeus into a more comfortable position and leaving the smelly alley behind. "You haven't had enough excitement for one day?"

She flicked her wings in a shrug. "I'll grant your first day back has been more interesting than most."

"Well, I still have one last errand to run."

Aurelis made a grumbling sound deep in her chest.

"I'm thinking I need to upgrade my home security system." My security system currently consisted of a lock on the door and my hand weapons, but no need to mention that. "And I could use your impressive tech expertise."

I'd only recently learned that Aurelis *had* technological expertise, but I'd figured out long ago that she liked being admired for the knowledge she pursued and acquired at astonishing speeds.

(*I* might've acquired more knowledge too if she hadn't suckered me into doing all our paperwork in exchange for transporting me to and from emergency calls.)

Somewhat appeased, her eyes of liquid gold fixed on me with new interest. "Go on."

"We know that no human, shifter, vampire, or goblin mind is safe from Metcalf. And while his ability to coerce some of the less common supernaturals remains uncertain,

Gadson's offer to station a security detail outside my apartment is more likely to provide Metcalf with extra puppets for his dirty work than give me any real protection."

"*Dragons* are probably impervious. But I'm not volunteering to stand outside all night and listen to you snore. And I'm not letting you anywhere near my hoard either."

"Has anyone ever told you what a kind and supportive person you are?"

She huffed. "No."

"Huh. Mysteries never cease..." I smirked and dodged the wing tip she swiped in my direction. "The point is, however his magic works, I'm pretty sure it wouldn't work on an *artificial* mind. So I was thinking I should invest in a personal protection drone."

"In that case, you're going the wrong way."

"What? There's a huge drone store on Sands Avenue."

"You can't get an accredited AI drone. If its protocol follows Asimov's Second Law to obey your every order, then as soon as you're compromised, the drone will be useless to you. You need an AI that will *disobey* a direct order."

"Oh." The wind left my sails. I'd really thought I'd been onto something here. "Right."

"I know someone. Come on."

Aurelis led me to the colloquially coined "magic markets," which were *mostly* legal but far less regulated than traditional retail sellers. If you had a problem, someone had probably created a product that promised to solve it and crammed it into one of the overflowing stalls in the magic markets. Need paint that will resist attempts at graffiti? This one will dissolve any chemical put on it. Need spray paint to overcome a graffiti-resistant wall? Try our new Conquest range. Wade through garbage to collect your friend's dog? Our magic deodorizer will leave you smelling like sunlight. Want to forget it ever happened? Visit Jinja's booth and wipe your unpleasant memory as clean as your deodorized shoes.

Much of it was as dodgy as it sounded, but there were enough magic-powered miracles amid the junk to keep people coming back. Just one more way to roll the dice in the gambling capital of America.

The market was crowded like always, so I continued to carry Zeus so he wouldn't accidentally get stepped on. After a minute of winding through the press of bodies, merchandise, and some of the more aggressive vendors, Aurelis nudged me into a small shop I'd never noticed before. It was teeming with machine parts and wasn't much to look at, but the rent on a permanent shop space in the magic markets was steep, so the owner must be doing okay for themselves.

The being in question appeared no more hospitable than the state of her shop. She was five foot nothing and slightly built, with the slitted eyes of a predator and thin lips parted to show sharp, pointed teeth. Her skin was a dark shimmery blue, and five horns sprouted from her midnight hair like the top half of a mohawk. (I wondered briefly if the sharp, fixed spikes limited her sleeping positions.) Her two natural arms were folded across her chest in a stance that suggested she was unimpressed, while her two magitech arms continued doing something on the bench behind her. Whatever her species was, it wasn't one I'd encountered before.

She gave me the same once-over I was giving her, then waved one of her natural hands in lazy dismissal. "I don't take dog meat as payment anymore."

Her tone was too bored for it to be some kind of jest.

Any*more*? I clutched Zeus tight to my chest. "Um, that's fine," I squeaked.

Aurelis couldn't fit into the shop, but she'd poked her head in behind me, which meant I could *feel* her snort of amusement.

"Don't worry, Zax, she's not quite as wimpy as she looks. Lyra, tell her what you need."

I squared my shoulders, resolved not to set Zeus down until we were well clear of the market, and started talking.

The shopkeeper Zax listened to my unusual list of requirements and then flashed her pointed teeth in a way that was not at all heartening.

"I have just the thing." She gestured around the cluttered shop.

"You're currently surrounded by thirty miniature stealth drones with different individual defense specialties operated by a single AI. The beauty of using an

unorthodox system is that your enemy can't take coun-
teractive measures against something they haven't
anticipated. Miniature drone systems are harder to see,
harder to disable, and still almost unheard of in today's
market. I call it Hive. And like all my AIs, this one is
miles ahead of anything they're selling at Drone
World, well capable of carrying out complex procedures independently. Hell, for the right price, I can
even provide you with someone able to monitor your
goings-on and control the AI externally from a secure
location on another continent. By the time your
enemy realizes you're protected by a team of miniature
drones that *you* don't command, they'll have already
lost."

Holy smokes. That sounded better than anything I'd
thought to hope for. So much better, in fact, that I
might even be able to sleep at night.

Better some security guy on another continent
watch me sleep than a psychopath in my bedroom.

Time and distance were two of the few constraints
Metcalf's magic had.

My wide, roaming gaze had still failed to spot a
single one of the miniature stealth drones.

"That sounds great. How much?"

She named her price. And despite my earlier resolution, I almost dropped Zeus in shock. I took an unconscious step backward and bumped into Aurelis's nose.
"Ah, that might be out of my budget." Even if I sold
every possession I owned, lived off instant ramen, and

maxed out my credit cards. "Do you have anything cheaper?"

"How much cheaper?"

I mean, we were talking about my life here, but I had to be honest. "I need the shoestring version."

It was a sad fact of the justice system that criminals made more than cops did. Aurelis never seemed short on money, but then maybe she'd inherited a cave of gold or something.

Zax pulled her thin bottom lip between her sharp teeth. "I have an experimental prototype that needs field testing. If you document your experience, I can loan it to you for a ten-day for a pittance."

The price sounded good, but— "Experimental?" I asked dubiously. This was my life we were gambling with.

"Zax is *extremely* talented," Aurelis said. "I'd prefer to use something she's throwing out than the latest model of anything in the usual stores."

I wasn't sure I'd ever heard Aurelis heap that much praise on anyone besides herself. It was oddly bolstering. "Okay. Show me."

Zax disappeared behind several towers of precariously stacked machinery and returned with an underwhelming-looking drone under one arm. Four small propellers, a few retracted gun barrels, some more accessories I didn't recognize... But overall it looked more like a kid's toy than something you'd stake your life on.

"I call her Strike. Her armor and weapons are top-notch, although some of those are experimental too, but it's her AI that's most untried. She has more... personality, more curiosity, than the average drone. Curiosity-driven learning leads to more advanced and creative problem-solving rather than following the usual formulaic procedures. So answering any questions she has should increase performance. Plus the more she knows about you, the more easily she'll be able to determine when you're acting against your will."

"Okaaay," I said cautiously, trying to conceal my skepticism.

"I'll have to tweak her programming a little. Hang on."

I looked around for somewhere to sit while we waited, but there wasn't anywhere. So I settled for petting Zeus instead.

I'd barely started on his favorite spots before Zax announced, "All done." She handed me the inert drone, and I searched for the power switch.

"Um, maybe wait to power her on in a less crowded area the first time she wakes up."

Even *less* reassured, I shifted Zeus to one arm and took the drone under the other. Then forced myself to smile brightly. "Thank you."

"Just make sure you write the reports. And answer her questions."

More paperwork. If Metcalf didn't kill me, the paperwork would.

CHAPTER SEVEN

Stewie was looking considerably worse than when we'd last spoken. I'd managed to wrangle him a private holding cell usually reserved for the extra rich or extra dangerous, but he was sitting rigid against the wall, fingers gripping his own arms so tight his fingernails were gouging the skin. And his eyes were flicking back and forth, scanning for some imminent threat that didn't exist.

I plonked the drone down outside the holding cell and went in.

His eyes latched onto me but didn't soften the way they usually did, and for a split second, I feared I'd miscalculated. But then Zeus barked and wriggled to be let down, and Stewie's feverish tension drained away like water from an overturned bucket.

The little dog bounded across the room and straight

into Stewie's lap. A tear rolled down my CI's weathered cheek.

I gave them a minute and then squatted down beside them. "Why did the dragon cross the road?"

Stewie's face creased in a smile. It was a question he often asked to prove it was really me when we spoke over the phone, and I always chided him for being inappropriate.

"I dunno, boss. Why?"

I flashed my teeth. "To get the bastard who did this." I gripped his shoulder for a moment. "We're retracing everyone's steps leading up to this morning's incidents, hoping to get surveillance footage of the guy responsible. As soon as we can confirm you're no longer under his influence, I should be able to get you released on bail. But I hope Zeus will help you be comfortable here until then."

Stewie's eyes stayed on the dog.

"Thanks, boss."

"You're very welcome, Stewie."

I pushed to my feet and let myself out of the cell.

Now I just had to clear it with Gadson.

A couple of hours later, I'd finished writing up my reports and was about to head out for the day when the captain pinned me down. He'd agreed to let Zeus stay in the cell, and I was hoping he wasn't coming to tell me he'd changed his mind.

"What are you doing about your safety tonight?" he asked instead.

I told him about the drone, and he looked faintly reassured.

Probably because I didn't tell him *all* about the drone.

Aurelis agreed to escort me home, so I decided to wait until I got there to power Strike up.

I was going to have enough trouble without a potentially malfunctioning artificial intelligence peppering me with questions—or doing whatever Zax had been worried about when she warned me not to turn Strike on in the market. Ronan was due to send a car for my family in less than an hour, and I hadn't even broached the topic of an impromptu family holiday in Faerie with Dad yet.

"Would you mind keeping an eye on things here until my family is safely on their way?"

Aurelis's huge and haughty presence made me feel far more secure than my untried drone. But I knew I was asking a lot. My apartment building wasn't sized for dragons, and she had no real interest in my father or younger siblings. Why should she? Her sole experience of "family" was being left to hatch and fend for herself before she was even out of the egg. Dragons were solitary creatures that formed deep relational bonds with their hoards and little else. Blood ties were so unimportant that family names didn't even exist in their society.

I glanced at the almost imperceptible scratches on her copper scales left by the hail of bullets from Stewie's submachine gun. Bullets she'd taken at my request.

"I'll buy you an annual pass to the Scale Spa?"

A wisp of smoke escaped her maw. "You're testing my magnanimity, human."

I bit back a grin. She wouldn't be mad if she wasn't staying. "Thank you. You're the best."

I hightailed it up to the third floor before she could change her mind and eat me.

My family's apartment was just a couple of doors down from mine. Close enough that I could help out and see them regularly. Far enough that various supernatural ears wouldn't overhear when I had company over.

I knocked and let myself in.

Instead of being swamped by younger siblings and wading through them to reach my father, I found him sitting in the living room alone.

It was rare to see him that way. Miles was most in his element when he was meeting the needs of others. Whether it was juggling the care, feeding, and entertainment of three young supernaturals—something his vampiric speed, strength, and minimal sleep requirements made him uniquely suited to—or listening with his full attention as one of his wards poured out their struggles.

But his bright smile of greeting when he saw me allayed any fears that something might be wrong. He sprang off the couch to give me a hug.

"What are the kids up to?" I asked while I soaked in the comfort of those familiar arms.

"Playing hide-and-seek."

Hide-and-seek was not played the traditional way in the Ridley household. Blake and Archer had noses far too good at sniffing someone out within the confines of the apartment, and as natural predators, all they ever wanted to do was do the seeking. Or the *stalking* and *hunting* as they preferred to call it. Definitely *not* the hiding. Which meant that role had always fallen to poor Sage.

Until the three of them had come up with the bright alternative where they combined their wits to find a new and superb hiding place for that day's designated object. Then Miles wiped the last few minutes of their memories, and they *all* got to be the hunters.

Ta-da. Three happy kids entertained for a good ten minutes.

Miles hadn't been entirely comfortable with the proposal. All vampires had the ability to erase the last few minutes from someone's memory—a useful defense mechanism in the centuries before blood bags were freely available.

Instead of being chased out of every village by angry, pitchfork-wielding folks, you could go to the local watering hole, buy your target a few drinks (a drink for a drink and all that), coax them out somewhere quiet, take a modest amount of blood, and then make them forget that last part ever happened. The target would chalk up their brief memory glitch and the weakness from their unwitting blood donation to drinking too much. Which sure beat the pitchfork thing.

These days, of course, none of that was necessary.

Miles had made no attempt to conceal the facts from us kids, but he'd promised each of us he would never use that ability on family. However, for all their differences —Sage's gentleness, Blake's studiousness, and Archer's enthusiasm—and the lack of any biological relation, my three younger siblings did share one trait.

Stubbornness.

And in the end, they'd worn Dad down on the subject. Even single parents blessed with the advantages of being a vampire gave way under the pressure of determined young minds on occasion.

I knew Miles had honored the spirit of his promise though. Because the day I'd accidentally caught him at the hospital and learned that my seemingly invincible vampire parent who'd walked the earth for almost three hundred years was dying, it would've been a simple matter to wipe my memory of running into him. Instead, he'd bought me a crappy hot chocolate from the hospital cafeteria and told me everything.

Told me that he had a neurological disease that was going to kill him. Slowly but inevitably over the space of about ten years. And before it killed him, it was going to erase him. Bit by bit, it would eat away at the neurons in his brain, gradually rendering him unable to remember who he was. Unable to remember the family he'd worked so hard to build. Unable to remember how to speak, how to move and, one day a decade from now, how to breathe.

Sometimes I wished he *had* wiped my memory.

But he hadn't. And I was determined to savor every moment we still had. To not hurt him further, steal from him faster, by coloring our remaining time together with my grief.

So I stepped back from the shelter of his arms and took him in. The man who'd raised me with such love and kindness and the sort of patience that could only be borne from centuries of experience. He looked no older now than he did in my baby pictures. At 284, his face was young—mid-thirties by human standards—and almost boyish with a generous sprinkling of freckles and only the faintest of lines. Despite everything he'd witnessed and endured over his long years, his blue eyes were more often laughing than grave, and his mop of dark red hair remained stubbornly resistant to any form of discipline.

My mind flashed unwillingly to the moment that hair had been gripped by hostile hands in this same living room, wrenched backward to expose his vulnerable throat.

I swallowed.

I had to get them out of Metcalf's reach.

"We have to talk."

My father gave me an assessing look. "Is this about that phone call earlier today?"

"Yes. Sort of." Far out, it felt so, so long ago. "I need you and the kids to leave the city." I launched into the rundown of why, speaking fast and quiet to decrease the chance of my siblings listening in. "So I've arranged for you to stay in Faerie."

An odd expression flitted over Miles's face. "And they've agreed to it? Does your fae friend know that your adoptive parent's a vampire?"

"Yes, why?"

He shook his head. "I don't like this, milksucker. Isn't risking everything to save the city once already enough for... I don't know, another couple of weeks at least?"

"You know what, that's a good point. I'll ask the bad guys to lay off for another week, shall I?"

I bumped his shoulder with mine.

"Perhaps you should rethink raising such competent kids if you don't like it. If you hadn't taught me to care about others and given me the skills and confidence to stand up for myself, I might be perfectly happy to sit on my hands while others do the hard stuff."

Miles had trained us all in self-defense from an early age. And he'd managed to do it in such a way that made us feel empowered and safe rather than fearful of the world.

It was only as I'd gotten older that I'd seen through

the cracks. That as well as he camouflaged it, that need to train us came from a time in his life he wouldn't talk about. A time he hadn't been able to protect himself or someone he loved. Being homosexual and a redhead and a vampire had been a threefold death sentence over much of his existence.

And after that, I'd started noticing how much of his life was dedicated to shoring up some of the cracks in a world he considered broken.

I only loved him more for it.

But my wisecrack made him wince.

"I'll be careful, Dad. I acquired a personal protection drone to shadow me that won't be influenced by Metcalf's magic. And don't forget my partner's a *dragon*. If anyone can tackle Metcalf, it's Aurelis."

I hoped she heard that from wherever she was waiting outside. Her ego could do with some buttering up.

I could see Miles force himself to back down. He wasn't a helicopter parent. He let us make our own decisions, our own messes. But he was always there to help with the fallout.

"How much school will the kids miss out on?"

I'd already thought about that.

"We both know Sage could use the break." From the bullying, I meant. She had the misfortune of wearing some of her uniqueness on the outside in the form of two horns sprouting from her curls. And after thousands of years of evolution, humankind still hadn't learned that different didn't need to be considered threatening or inferior.

As the dominant species on earth, that lesson had been optional.

"Archer will probably learn more running around a whole new country than he would being forced to sit at a desk," I continued. "And Blake is plenty capable of continuing his studies without assistance."

Miles eyed me with suspicion. "Is there a reason you had all this time to plan this conversation and not enough time to give me more notice it was coming?"

"Think of it as a holiday," I advised. I nudged him again. "I even made Ronan promise to arrange for someone else to do all the cooking."

My father gave me a long-suffering look. He excelled at many aspects of parenthood, but as someone who subsisted on blood alone, cooking wasn't one of them. "Honestly, do you know how many starving people over the centuries would've been fervently thankful for a humble meal? You act like I'd serve you rotten meat with broken glass sprinkled on top."

I screwed my face up in thought. "That *might* taste better," I allowed.

He swatted me.

I grinned. "See? Now you won't even miss me while you're gone."

CHAPTER EIGHT

A black Mercedes G-Class with plates in a design I'd never seen before arrived as Miles and the kids were running around throwing things into suitcases.

Blake finished first. "All done," he announced and flopped onto his bed to continue reading.

I picked up the suitcase. Well, *tried* to pick up the suitcase. It didn't budge. "What on earth do you have in here?" I complained.

Blake didn't look up. "My books and cairn stones."

Ever since he'd read a historic account about the curse that befell any who dared to remove a stone from the ancient burial cairns in Scotland, this had been Blake's funerary preference of the week. He liked the idea of a mysterious guardian watching over his resting place long, long after he was gone. And he'd promptly begun selecting rocks for his own burial cairn.

I unzipped the lid and peered inside. "Are you sure

you need all of these? They have books and rocks in Faerie too."

"Don't worry," Miles called from Sage's room. "I'll carry it."

I took a second look at the bag's contents. "Do you have any clothes in here?"

Blake shrugged. "I'm sure they have clothes in Faerie too."

Touché, kid.

I sighed, tossed a few complete outfits on top, and zipped it back up.

"Archer, how are you coming along?"

I turned around and saw only his abandoned suitcase, still mostly empty with just his sword and video games sticking out of it. Then someone knocked on the apartment door, and Archer's excited voice trickled back to me.

"Hi! Are you Ronan? Can you fly? Can I touch your wings? Can you give me wings? What's it like in Faerie? Is it true the trees are made of cotton candy?"

Was it Ronan? I hadn't been sure whether he'd send someone or come himself.

Either way, I should rescue the poor unfortunate.

Wincing, I glanced down to remind myself what state I was in—my uniform still smelled faintly of garbage and appeared to have sprouted a layer of wiry black dog fur—then edged out into the living room.

Ronan's intense dark gaze met mine over Archer's head, and something within me sparked in response.

"I'm afraid not," he said. "The trees are made of normal things."

Not all of them, I knew. The hedge around the prison had almost killed me.

Archer glanced at me, disappointment written all over his face at the news that the trees would not be edible.

"But you could ask the cook to make you cotton candy," Ronan offered.

"I'd advise against it," I said. "Archer has plenty of energy without loading him up on sugar." I fixed my brother with my sternest look. "Speaking of, why don't you use some of that energy to finish packing?"

He groaned theatrically and trudged back to his room. Well, he started out trudging. But within five strides of this expressive demonstration, his boundless energy and happy-go-lucky nature won out, and he bounce-skipped the rest of the way.

I walked over to Ronan, who was still standing in the doorway, and ushered him inside. As evinced by Archer's line of questioning, he'd opted not to conceal his wings today.

Damn. They were even more drool-worthy than I remembered. It really seemed unfair that they coexisted with his lithe, muscular form and striking face of hard planes, arresting eyes, and soft, inviting lips. Worse, he smelled better than any man had a right to—like clean soap and caramelized butter and ancient untouched forest—and I knew exactly what the abs concealed beneath his shirt felt like.

"Thank you for coming. It wasn't necessary to escort them yourself."

Fae magic was so deeply intertwined with the land of Faerie that beyond its borders they were left incomplete, weakened, vulnerable. Which was why I'd never met a fae until Ronan showed up in the Mojave Desert a couple of weeks ago and introduced himself.

And why pursuing any sort of long-term relationship with him was inadvisable.

"I deemed it necessary. Besides, I have other business in the city."

I blinked. "You do?" He'd once mentioned he'd only ever ventured outside of Faerie on one other occasion—and that he hadn't liked it. So what business could he have in the city?

"Yes. I wanted to see for myself that you'd survived the past week without my company."

I stared at him. He was joking, right? I assumed he was joking. He couldn't know of all the times I'd thought about those hours on the back of his motorcycle, riding with my chest pressed against his feathers and my arms wrapped around his waist...

And I didn't even *like* motorcycles.

Once again I hoped the fae didn't secretly have mind-reading magic.

"That's funny, I seem to recall saving *you* rather than the other way around." He did not look pleased at the reminder. "But I'm good. I haven't gotten a feather stuck up my nose once."

His lips twitched. "How relieving to hear."

I grinned. "What about you? I hope it wasn't too much trouble to arrange last-minute visas for my family's stay?"

He glanced away. "Less trouble than you took on to rescue the people of Las Vegas and Faerie's honor."

Yikes. "That bad, huh? What'd you have to do? Promise the border authorities your firstborn?"

His continued aversion to meeting my eyes sent a trickle of guilt through me. He hadn't needed to offer me a favor. Yes, my actions had helped Faerie, but I hadn't done it for them.

"That might've been preferable," he muttered.

Before I could dig deeper to find out just *how* guilty I ought to feel, he asked, "Is your older sister coming too?"

I'd called Kaida in New York and Dimitri in Antarctica to update them on the situation and invite them to have a holiday in Faerie too. It was no surprise Dimitri had turned me down. I figured he was pretty safe, isolated where he was in a part of Antarctica nearly inaccessible this time of year. Kaida had turned me down as well, which also wasn't surprising. But I wished she'd reconsider. She was strong, independent, and more than capable of looking after herself under normal circumstances, but Metcalf only needed to hop on one short plane ride to get to New York.

"Unfortunately not," I said.

Miles entered the living room with Sage peering shyly around his legs.

"Ronan, meet my dad, Miles Ridley, who I blame entirely for the way I've turned out, and my little sister Sage. Guys, this is Lord Ronan Nightwing, who I worked with to take down the dome."

I scooped Sage up so she could be more or less on the same level as the rest of us. She was six years old, half faun, half human, and ridiculously cute with the gentlest of hearts and the hardest of heads.

"Ronan, most people don't know, but this courageous girl single-handedly saved my family from a knife-wielding grown man three times her size. And in doing so, she saved the entire city, because her brave act gave me the strength and courage I needed to take down everyone inside that ranch house."

Ronan bowed gravely. "It is an honor to meet you, Lady Sage."

She blushed as dark as her skin allowed, but thus bolstered, she reached out slowly and traced the bottom of Ronan's wing with one delicate fingertip.

I suspected Ronan was regretting his decision to leave his wings on display, but to his credit, his expression remained stoic and he didn't twitch them out of reach.

Miles inclined his head. "Thank you for your aid and hospitality." But while his words and gesture were polite, the smile didn't reach his eyes the way it usually did. "I'm aware vampires are rarely welcome in Faerie."

My head snapped between him and Ronan. They weren't? I'd never heard that.

But then I'd never researched Faerie as a travel destination either. And it wasn't like I knew even a fraction of the ancient history between fae and vampires—or most of the other supernatural species for that matter.

Now didn't seem the time to ask.

Ronan returned the nod. "You are welcome." He placed a slight emphasis on the *you* as if to exclude all others of Dad's kind. "I've witnessed enough of your daughter's character to trust you won't be a threat to us."

Was that a compliment?

Wait. A *threat*? To the fae? In Faerie?

Beyond Faerie's borders, a fae's magic was versatile but limited. *Within* Faerie, however, they were almost invulnerable, and there was very little they couldn't do. That and their unrivaled border security was why I believed my family would be safe there. Even from the likes of Metcalf.

"I hope you will be comfortable at my estate."

I was glad no one was looking at me just then because my eyes might've bugged out of my head. *Ronan's* estate?

As much as I'd love to see where Ronan called home, he didn't exactly give off friendly host vibes.

"I, uh, thought you'd just put them up at a nice hotel," I ventured.

"It's better this way," Ronan said. "Easier to protect them."

"And easier to protect others from me," Miles stated quietly.

Another acknowledgment passed between them. "That and the only way I could get them into Faerie today was as my personal guests."

My guilt increased. I imagined Ronan's serene and orderly house—because I'd bet my last clean uniform that his home was serene and orderly—turned upside down by the chaotic forces of my younger siblings.

As if to validate my concerns, Archer charged out from the bedroom, dragging a reluctant Blake after him. "See, that's him!" Archer exclaimed. "Do you think he knows how to use a sword? Do you think he'll let me practice on him? I hope he has a castle. With a moat. With alligators!"

Blake gazed at Ronan appraisingly. "Cool wings," he said. "Did you know that in some cultures the black wings of a raven are considered a harbinger of death?"

Well, at least he hadn't asked his favorite question about what sort of funerary rites Ronan would prefer in the event of his *inevitable death*.

Ronan's expression was resolute, like he might actually be fantasizing about his death just now.

"I'll see how the boys are getting along with their packing," I chirped.

CHAPTER NINE

My family departed with Ronan half an hour later. I mirrored the enthusiastic waves goodbye given to me by my siblings and tried not to wish I was going with them. I prayed they'd be safe. And wondered at exactly what Ronan had had to do to make them so.

As bargained, Aurelis was still waiting nearby. She'd been sitting out here twiddling her talons for over an hour.

I'd rarely known her to wait patiently for anything except when it came to acquiring a rare collector's edition of a book she coveted. Which meant either the book she was reading was *really* good, or she was more concerned for me than she'd ever let on.

Or—I swallowed, remembering my promise to tell her about my newly acquired magic—maybe she'd waited to ensure I kept my word.

"Thanks for sticking around," I said, just on the off

chance it was for the protection thing rather than the interrogation thing. "I owe you an explanation about, um, what happened on that rooftop."

She tossed her head. "You do," she agreed. "But I have better things to do right now, and your big secret is probably not that interesting anyway. Just try not to die until tomorrow, hey?"

"Oh." Relief washed through me. Followed closely by suspicion. My dragon friend—who thirsted after knowledge, had no respect for personal boundaries, and few social graces—was leaving a juicy tidbit unturned? What on earth did she have on tonight? But I was exhausted, emotionally more than physically, although it made my limbs feel heavy all the same. If she wanted to defer this conversation, I was only too happy to oblige.

"Sure. Tomorrow then."

She shifted her weight to launch into the air, and the blissful fantasy I had of flopping down on my couch in my quiet apartment acquired an undesirable edge. I flung out a hand.

"Um, sorry, but would you mind waiting around for just one more minute? I'll go upstairs and power up the drone to make sure it works, then text you the all clear. If I don't... Well, you know. Send in the SWAT team, bash down the building, all that good stuff."

She snorted. "Sure. I live to serve."

"Remind me why you decided to become a cop again?" It was a question she'd never given me a real answer to, and after six months, I was no closer to getting to the bottom of it than the first day we'd met.

She eyeballed me. "Nice try."

I jogged up to my apartment, switched on the drone, and helped myself to a big bowl of ice cream while it powered up. In general, I ate pretty healthily, but after the day I'd had, I figured I'd earned some comfort food.

"Hello, Lyra. You may call me Strike. I will be your personal protection drone." Her voice was measured and soothing, like looking after my mental well-being was all part of the package.

"Hi, Strike," I replied dutifully before spooning another delicious mouthful of gooey sweetness into my mouth.

"My sources confirm the local time as six thirteen in the evening. Do you always eat ice cream for dinner?"

Not in the mood to justify my life choices to an AI who didn't have taste buds and therefore would never understand the temptation, I shut my eyes and enjoyed the mundane miracle of how the cold stuff on my tongue could fire up the pleasure center in my brain.

I knew I'd agreed to answer her questions, but surely she could wait awhile.

The quiet whir of her propellers drew closer, and then my ice cream bowl was snatched out of my hand. My eyes snapped open, and I watched in disbelief as the drone lugged my self-indulgent dessert to the kitchen via a retractable arm I'd had no idea she possessed and dumped the entire bowl in the trash.

I gaped at her—it.

"What the hell?"

"I am programmed to protect you from any action that may lead to physical harm. Even self-inflicted harm," she informed me in the same calm, measured tone as before. Except now instead of being soothing, it made me want to throw something.

After a second, I threw the spoon, and it clunked satisfyingly off her armored hull.

"Change your settings then!" I growled. "You may protect me from any action leading to *imminent* physical harm."

"Imminent is a nebulous parameter. Define imminent."

"I don't know. Something less than *fifty* years?" I drawled.

"Setting updated."

"No. Wait!" I thought about it. I wanted to say five minutes, but what if Metcalf figured out that parameter and found a way around it? "Make it any action leading to foreseeable grievous physical harm within a period of two weeks."

"Okay. Setting updated. For your personal safety, you may not update any further settings for one thousand minutes."

"Can you at least update your settings to translate that to a more human-normative time frame?"

"Negative."

I thunked my head against the dining table. "Great."

Something about banging my head against a solid object made me remember to text Aurelis. *Before* she could assemble a SWAT team or smash down the wall to "rescue" me.

"You did not answer my question earlier," Strike said, her propellers bringing her closer. "Do you always eat ice cream for dinner?"

"No. It has just been a very rough day, all right? Some species like to eat sugary food for comfort."

Strike processed this. "Would you like to see a video of the visceral fat excavated from a human corpse's abdominal cavity after a lifetime of consuming excess sugar?"

"No. Would you drop the subject already?"

"I sense I have bothered you. But I am programmed to question any action that might lead to your physical harm. Even self-inflicted harm."

I sighed and forced myself to go to the kitchen and find something for my actual dinner. As much as I wanted ice cream over a preachy, overbearing drone, I needed Strike to question my actions, or she'd be useless as soon as Metcalf sank his hooks into my mind. I forced myself to focus on the positive. She was obviously intelligent, even if she wasn't *smart*. My family should be safe in Faerie by now. Stewie was cuddled up with Zeus. Tomorrow Aurelis and I would join the team hunting

Metcalf. And as soon as we caught the bastard, I could return Strike to Zax.

That last bit finally drained some of my tension.

I opened the fridge. I was a better cook than Miles but not by as much as I'd like. I settled on throwing together a simple chicken salad and shoveled it down, trying to answer Strike's questions with a little more grace.

What are the known exits and entrances to the apartment? What was my usual routine? Could I provide a list of expected visitors? What self-defense skills did I possess? Why had I chosen a teal-colored couch? Why didn't I have a pet? Or a houseplant? Was it indicative of my ability to keep other living things alive? What did feelings feel like? Would I prefer to be a tiger or a llama? What—when I went to fetch clean clothes—*was the rationale behind humans wearing pajamas?*

I fled into the bathroom for a shower, already fantasizing about escaping into sleep. My head felt like it had been stuffed full of what-ifs and thrown into the dryer on an unending tumble cycle. I was stressed. I was worn out. And I'd had enough of both my personal protection drone's and my own unanswerable questions for one day.

Clean and comfortable in my apparently irrational pajamas, I exaggerated a yawn and told Strike, "I'm going to sleep now. Please wake me if anything suspicious happens overnight."

"This is a deviation from your usual routine. Is this

cause for concern? What time do you expect to sleep until?"

She made a tsking noise when I gave her the time, allowing myself a generous nine hours of sleep.

"Humans need to charge for so long. It's most inefficient."

"Good night to you too," I grumbled and flung back the bedcovers. Where I noticed an unmarked envelope waiting for me on my pillow.

My drowsiness evaporated. Replaced by apprehension.

I went to the kitchen and grabbed a large Ziploc bag and a pair of single-use, food-safe gloves as a make-do forensics kit.

"What are you doing?" Strike asked. "I thought you were going to bed? Do you wear gloves to bed?"

I ignored her, wondering if I was being paranoid. Maybe Miles or Sage had left it for me. They both had keys to my apartment. And I hadn't seen any sign of forced entry.

Then again, Metcalf could doubtless convince the building super to let him in.

I eased the envelope open with Strike whirring over my shoulder.

It was an autopsy report.

For a toddler.

Human. Female. Caucasian. Thirteen months old. Identified as Ruby Miller aka test subject A31438B.

In the Probable Cause of Death box, the medical

examiner had written: *Brain hemorrhage. Consistent with complications from the experimental procedure for the Lyrebird project.*

And across the top of the page, he'd scrawled an additional note. *Final test subject to die. Mortality rate for procedure 100%.*

But the thing that caught and held my attention was one of the attached photos. The child had been photographed front and back, left and right. And on her shaved scalp above her left ear was a small scar in a perfect square.

Exactly like the one above *my* left ear. A peculiar scar I'd only discovered during an unfortunate phase where I'd thought an undercut would look good on me.

Acid burned the back of my throat. My cozy illusion of safety shattered. Metcalf could've gotten me this report in a myriad of ways. He'd chosen this one because he wanted me to know he'd been in my apartment. To know that he'd violated the sanctuary of my home. That he'd come and gone without anyone noticing.

And could come again whenever he wanted.

I stared at the sheet of paper some more. The date of the autopsy was twenty-one years ago. I would've been about thirteen months old at the time. The same age as Ruby Miller. Hell, if I didn't know better, I could've sworn she *was* me. Same coloring. Same face shape. Same age. Same scar.

Numbly, I searched for the print Dimitri had sent me a while back—an old family photo of me, him, and

Kaida gathered around a kneeling, grinning, sopping-wet Miles on one of our frequent trips to the local salt-water swimming pool for my arctic selkie brother. I was about two at the time and wearing a bright yellow life jacket almost as large as I was. The dead girl in the autopsy was similar enough she could've been my twin.

I looked at the date again. Miles never hid the facts from us. We all knew we were adopted, no matter what age we'd been adopted at. And we all knew he loved us as much as any child who might've shared his blood. Or at least, he proved it to us time and time again until we finally believed that.

As a result, we each celebrated two dates every year. Our birthday, or our estimated birthday as it was in my case, and the day we'd joined the family.

The autopsy date was several days before a minister had found me on the steps of his church in Laughlin. Bundled up against the cold of the desert night with no identification whatsoever except a scrap of paper saying that my name was Lyra. Had my head been shaved like the girl's in the photo? I didn't know. Miles had taken me in three months later, and by the time I was old enough for him to tell me the details of my "discovery," I'd been too content in my new life to care.

Sure, I'd wondered every now and then, but not enough to do anything about it. Adoption was so normalized in my family that I didn't feel lost or unusual or even overly curious. My older sister had known her biological family, and her experience with them had ensured I'd counted my blessings. My career in the police force had only cemented that. There were plenty of people capable of reproducing that should never have been parents. And their stories were common and repetitive enough that they no longer aroused my interest. I was infinitely grateful I'd landed in Miles's vampiric lap.

Now, for the first time in my life, curiosity awoke in my chest.

What could this mean?

And why on earth was someone, presumably Metcalf, drawing my attention to it?

It took me longer than it should have to find the handwritten note scrawled on the back of one of the photos.

After your inconvenient defeat of eight of my loyal followers, I was intrigued about you and your magic. How had you pulled it off? And could I harness your abilities for my own ends? So I did some digging.

Imagine my surprise when I found out you're supposed to be dead...

CHAPTER TEN

Maybe it was a trap, but if so, it was one I couldn't resist triggering.

I ran a search for the name Ruby Miller in the police database. No applicable results. I searched for her in the magic database. No results. That wasn't surprising for someone who hadn't made it to puberty. I searched for her in the Vital Records archive. Someone by that name had been born at a community clinic in Phoenix, Arizona, in the right month and year to link up to the girl in the autopsy report. But despite the document I held in my hand, there was no corresponding registration of her death.

Why not?

No father was listed on the birth record, but her mother's name was Amethyst Miller. I searched the online news archives for both names over the subsequent years and eventually found one short article about how twenty-seven-year-old mother Amethyst Miller had told police that someone had stolen her three-week-old baby girl after community workers reported the infant as missing. Miller was a known drug addict, and authorities feared for the child's safety.

There was no follow-up. That early in the tumultuous years following the magic revolution, it was surprising one missing child of a drug addict was enough to make the news at all.

Could that missing girl really be me?

It seemed absurd. Especially when I had her apparent autopsy report right in front of me. And yet her features were so like mine, and that peculiar scar...

Ignoring the uncomfortable feelings the information stirred in me—information I'd never expected or wanted to learn—I ran through the medical examiner's name next.

My bio mother's name might be Amethyst Miller.

I typed the doctor's name into the search box and hit enter.

Her life had been rough enough that she'd felt like she needed brain-altering substances to survive it.

I scanned the results, narrowing them down to possible matches that fit with my timeline.

There was a possibility she may not have intentionally given me up.

I scowled at myself and tried to focus on the remaining results.

There was an equal possibility that she'd sold me to some ruthless entity to pay for her next fix.

No, dammit. I was looking into the medical examiner now.

The medical examiner who'd been involved in a highly suspect experimental procedure boasting a hundred percent mortality rate. *The Lyrebird project.*

A project this girl, who might be me, had been a test subject in.

Except I was still alive.

Did that mean Stewie's crazy-sounding theory about my oddball magic being the result of experimental tampering might be true?

Crazy-sounding, yes, and yet possessing another man's magic after killing him with it was crazy too.

None of this made sense.

The medical examiner—or neurosurgeon rather— had plenty of results.

He'd been educated and completed his neurological surgery residency at UC Davis in Sacramento. His magic ability complemented his profession—giving him greatly enhanced fine motor control. There were records of his working for at least six different organizations over the twenty-odd years of his career. And his last known residence was just outside San Bernardino, California.

San Bernardino was about three hours away.

Less by dragon flight.

I knew I should call this in. Should sit back and wait

for someone else to make sense of it, wait for proper procedure. But something made me hesitate.

My earlier fatigue had vanished, replaced with jittery tension. I had no hope of falling asleep now.

And maybe it was dumb, but my gut was telling me this was *personal*. Deeply personal. More so than anything else that had happened today. And I was reluctant to share whatever earth-shattering revelations the neurosurgeon might reveal with whichever officers Gadson happened to send.

Plus the proper procedures would take time. We'd have to jump through interstate jurisdiction hoops and wait for normal business hours for a start.

Aurelis and I could get there and back tonight.

Of course, first I'd have to fill her in. On everything this time. And hope she didn't squash me like a stink bug for not telling her earlier.

I called Aurelis. "Fancy a late-night adventure?"

It wasn't that late, only eight o'clock. I really *had* gone to bed early to avoid Strike.

"This better be good," she grumbled, but she didn't hang up.

Why did the dragon cross the road? Chances were good the real answer was because she was helplessly nosy.

I eyed the similarly curious drone I'd tricked into powering down. I'd been concerned she'd claim she couldn't be shut off for my own safety, and she might have a point. But I didn't know if she'd keep my secrets from Zax, and what I was about to do was crossing a lot of lines.

I drew in a deep breath and started talking.

Aurelis listened with an uncharacteristic lack of interruptions.

When I was done, she summarized. "So let me get this straight. You've been lying to me for over a week—"

"Not lying, just not—"

"You somehow permanently acquired the magic of the guy you killed."

"I don't know that for sure—"

"You shared this development with your CI instead of your *partner* and learned you might be living proof of one of his conspiracy theories."

"That's not how it... I didn't *mean* to share—"

"You have a new lead on Metcalf that might explain his interest in you and are intentionally withholding this evidence from an active investigation."

"Well, not exactly. I mean, not yet. I—"

"And now you want me to throw the rulebook out the window and pay an unofficial visit to a man whose only known characteristic is that he was involved in some highly suspect testing that killed a bunch of people. With nothing to go on except an autopsy report about someone that might be you, provided by a known psychopath."

I really didn't have a comeback to that one. I wilted. "Yeah, that about sums it up."

"You'll owe me a favor. No questions asked."

I hesitated.

Good sense told me this was a bad deal. Aurelis's moral compass was stuck on "seems reasonable" and "dragons are always right." Plus wisdom dictated you should never go shopping when you're hungry and absolutely never bargain with a dragon when you're desperate. But… I *was* desperate.

"I have the right to refuse if it's illegal," I hedged.

She huffed. "See you in five. Try not to commit any felonies while you wait."

CHAPTER ELEVEN

I changed into a clean uniform, pulled my warmest, windproof clothes overtop, and brought the autopsy report with me. Aurelis had us in San Bernardino within the hour.

The neurosurgeon's residence was a large, gable-roofed home surrounded by the sort of lush and thriving garden that you'd never find in Vegas—not without magic making it possible anyway. The garden was meticulously maintained, probably by someone else.

It was later than was polite to pay a house call, but right then, being polite had been bumped from my priority list. I marched up the charming, meandering footpath and rapped on the hardwood door.

A minute later, it was opened by an ordinary-looking man in his early fifties with a neatly trimmed beard, black-framed glasses, and a slight paunch. He wore plaid pajamas and an irritated expression.

"What—?"

Fear flashed over his face, and he stumbled back half a step. Not an unusual reaction when I had Aurelis beside me, except I could've sworn it was my uniform that'd triggered him. So quickly I might've imagined it, he'd recovered and was giving us a pasted-on smile. "Officers, what can I do for you?"

"Dr. Yanders, I take it? I'm Officer Rid—"

"I don't need your names," he said quickly. "Tell me what you want, and I'll see if I can help. I was about to go to bed."

Okay, so he wanted to skip the niceties, did he? I thrust the autopsy report at him.

"We need information on the work you were involved with twenty-one years ago. The Lyrebird project."

The skin around his eyes tightened. "I'm bound by a nondisclosure agreement. Sorry I couldn't be of assistance."

He tried to shut the door, but I shoved my foot in the way.

"We're not done, Dr. Yanders."

His irritation was back. Underlaid with something else. Fear?

"I can't break an NDA without a court order. And the Las Vegas police have no jurisdiction here. Why would I talk to you?"

But I was frustrated too now. Shaken and unsettled and unable to go home until I got answers.

I jabbed my finger at the photo of the dead girl. "Because I have a scar exactly like hers, and two days after the date on her autopsy report, I was abandoned on the steps of a church in Laughlin. I need to know why."

Surprise softened his expression, and he closed his eyes. When he opened them again, a grim resolve seemed to settle over him. Like a man who'd always known fate would catch up with him.

"Come around the back. There's a folding patio door the dragon should fit through. Although you may not want her to hear what I have to say."

Aurelis and I exchanged glances and then traipsed around the garden. If this was a trap set up by Metcalf, Dr. Yanders shouldn't have tried so hard to get rid of us.

A generous patio stretched across the rear wall, leading inside to a large sitting room with ceilings high enough for Aurelis. Dr. Yanders folded back the glass doors and let us in, then squatted down beside a liquor cabinet.

"Want a glass?" he asked, selecting a bottle from the bottom of the tidy rack and pouring one for himself.

It was wine. Expensive wine. Fifteen-year-old Grange, to be precise.

The sort of wine you reserve for once-in-a-lifetime occasions like a fiftieth wedding anniversary or becoming a surgeon after twelve or more years of training. A bottle that, had he bought it new, he hadn't had cause to open in over a decade.

I didn't know what it meant that he'd opened it now,

but my growing disquiet far outweighed my interest in tasting it.

Still, thinking it might put him at ease, I said, "Sure, just a little, thanks." I might be wearing a uniform, but I wasn't here in an official capacity.

He looked at Aurelis uncertainly. "I could get you a, um, bowl?"

She stared back until he looked away. "Dragons have no need of liquid courage."

He poured another glass and lifted his own to his lips, gulping down a mouthful, then refilling it.

Yikes.

Did he always drink like this? But no, not even a neurosurgeon could afford a nightly bottle of Grange. And he had none of the telltale signs of long-term alcohol abuse. No broken capillaries on his nose or face. No tremors in his hands. No bloodshot eyes or flushed complexion. Nor had his breath smelled like a wine barrel when he'd opened the door.

He brought over our glasses and plonked himself down on one of the white linen couches. I hesitantly followed suit. Aurelis remained standing, positioning herself so she could keep watch while I focused on the conversation.

"The experiment was a disaster from the start," Dr. Yanders said. "It was about twelve months after the magic revolution, and they were trying to tap into the burgeoning market for increasing a human's powers by way of a magitech biochip implanted in the brain"—his eyes flicked to Aurelis—"made from dragon scale of all things."

He took another swig from his glass.

"The design was promising. As I understand it, part of a dragon's magic resistance comes from a mechanism where their scales absorb unbound magic and then repurpose it into making those scales even more impervious. The biochip harnessed this absorption capacity on a nanoscopic level as a sort of memory card storage of a magic's unique data. In addition, the chip allowed the test subjects' brains to access and comprehend said data in order to reproduce that magic with their own power. In practice, it meant a test subject could download a person's magic once via skin-to-skin contact and gain that ability forever."

He rubbed his face.

"But it was also a hundred percent lethal. From what I could tell, the human brain has not evolved to hold and wield any magic, let alone a dozen of them. The strain proved too much on both the biochip and the cerebrum."

Another swig. This time I joined him although in a more measured amount. My heart was pounding, and I couldn't think of a single thing to say to keep him talking. I certainly didn't taste the much-lauded vintage.

But he did not need prompting. He didn't even look up. Seemingly absorbed by the garnet liquid in his glass.

"I was fresh and anxious to prove myself, and the position was an important stepping-stone toward working for the company leading the way in neurological magitech advancements. So I turned a blind eye to where they were getting the test subjects from and the absurdly high mortality rates. Told myself they'd hired me for the job, and I was obligated to complete it."

He shrugged, like he was trying to dislodge the guilt. "Even so, it was a relief when the project was shut down. I was ordered to go. Said they didn't need me anymore. But one of the test subjects was still alive. The youngest."

He glanced at me, then back to his glass. "She seemed to be responding to the biochip better than anyone else. Probably because she was too young to really use her magic and so couldn't download or replicate others' yet either. I suspected the company would dispose of her, and I don't know"—he shrugged again—"maybe it was seeing so many die, maybe it was just a moment of insanity, but I knew there was one way I could give her a fighting chance."

His fingers whitened around the wine stem, but he met my gaze and held it.

"I removed what I safely could of the chip, doctored up an autopsy report, turned on the cremation chamber, and told my boss she'd died during the night. Then I left as ordered with the girl hidden in my suitcase. I dumped her outside a church as soon as I thought we were far enough away and kept going."

It felt like Aurelis had sat on me.

I was the girl in the photos.

Stewie was right. My magic was the result of an experiment.

An experiment I was the only survivor of.

Because Dr. Yanders had saved me.

This man of questionable morals, who'd turned a blind eye to further his own career and was involved in the deaths of however many coerced or nonconsenting test subjects had been part of the project, had saved my life.

My hands shook around my glass—worse than any drunk's, and I'd only taken a single sip. Whatever else Dr. Yanders had done, I owed him… something. Gratitude? A swift trip to a cell? Maybe both. Except the latter wasn't in my jurisdiction.

"Thank you."

He nodded and sagged in his chair like a deflating tire. Exhausted. But maybe relieved too. As if this had been a peculiar sort of confessional.

"I'm glad I got to meet you. I didn't know if you'd survive. The reversal was only partial at best." He cocked his head. "Did it leave any lingering changes? Is your magic unusual?" He grimaced. "Actually no, don't tell me."

I'd opened my mouth to answer but took another sip of the expensive wine I couldn't taste instead.

My magic was only a pale echo of what had been intended. Which meant… what? I'd been left with a partial biochip, and likely because of that, either my "memory storage" or my access to that storage was faulty. A fact that had in all probability saved my life.

Except when I'd killed the chain mage, something had somehow overridden that fault to forge a permanent link to that one specific magic ability.

Whatever had caused it, all of this was uncharted territory.

Yanders leaned toward me in sudden earnest. "There are people out there who'd be very interested to learn you're still alive. Especially if it was even partially successful. The company I was working for is defunct now, but the parent company is FutureCorp, and they have their fingers in every lucrative pie across the globe and contracts with everyone from the largest energy research entity in China through to the US military. Be very careful who you trust."

His warning sent a chill through me.

Even I'd heard of FutureCorp. It had dozens, probably hundreds, of subsidiary companies. And okay, who knew how much oversight the parent company had? But one of those subsidiaries had conducted an experiment that illicitly acquired at least some of their test subjects and had a hundred percent mortality rate—and apparently no one had noticed.

Was the whole conglomerate of FutureCorp that unethical?

Maybe Stewie's paranoia was rubbing off on me, but I was relieved now that Dr. Yanders had faked my death. Not only because it had kept me alive, but because, with luck, he might be one of only four people who knew the truth about my existence, including me. And suddenly that seemed important.

My eyes swept over my companions, the ones who shared my secret. After twenty-one years of silence and an awful lot of culpability, I wasn't worried Yanders would talk.

Aurelis? Aurelis was less predictable. But after she'd covered for me on the rooftop by hacking the security footage unasked, I was pretty sure she'd keep this secret too.

I couldn't tell what she was thinking. But I couldn't recall her ever staying quiet and motionless so long without her snout in a book.

The three of us in this room... and Metcalf.

Swallowing hard, I asked, "Has anyone else come to see you about the Lyrebird project recently? About me?"

The nearly empty glass he'd been turning in his hands stilled. "No."

He was lying. And I feared I knew why. But if he was anything like Stewie and the others, no amount of questioning would change his answer.

I stood up to leave.

"Thank you for your help," I said. "Now and twenty-one years ago. We won't take up any more of your time."

He nodded and stood up too. It was like he'd run out of words now, and his movements were stiff and slow, as if the conversation had aged him several decades.

I turned to open the folding doors for Aurelis.

Behind me, Yanders returned to the liquor cabinet for a refill. I heard him unlatch it and slide out one of the drawers, then he spoke again. "There's one more thing I need to tell you before you go."

I turned back. Just in time to see him raise the gun. "No!"

Aurelis was halfway outside. She spun, coiling to spring, but was too late.

Dr. Yanders's face stretched in a rictus of a smile.

"The devil says hi," he whispered.

Then he pulled the trigger and splattered his brains over the couch he'd just been sitting on.

CHAPTER TWELVE

My shaking hand was dialing 911 before my mind could finish processing what had happened.

Aurelis smacked it out of my hand. "Don't be a fool."

I gaped at her, then back at the bloody mess on the couch and carpet and... everywhere.

"You heard what he said," she growled. "We need to keep this between us."

"But—"

"He's already beyond saving. What does it matter to him if it takes a few more hours for his body to be discovered? Take your wineglass, wipe down the doors for fingerprints, and let's get out of here."

Woodenly, I obeyed. Only remembering to retrieve my phone from the floor after Aurelis prompted me.

The flight home did little to clear my head. She dropped me back at my apartment. Still shaken.

"Th-thanks, Aurelis. For everything."

The dragon grunted. "Just get some sleep. You look awful. And turn your damn drone back on, or I'll beat you with it."

Despite Aurelis's instructions, I did not get much sleep.

I scrubbed myself down in the shower for far longer than necessary—like the inside of Dr. Yanders's head had somehow landed on me and was refusing to wash off. All the while, Strike peppered me with unhelpful questions about my "distressed state." And when I finally did fall into a fitful doze, she woke me up twice to report "suspicious activity" that turned out to be the neighbor's cat yowling in triumph after using its litter box and a late-night pizza delivery across the hall for someone who likely had the munchies.

All too soon and yet not nearly soon enough, it was time to get up.

Strike escorted me to work, with some misgivings on my part. She flew menacingly at a passerby who'd looked at me "for a suspicious length of time." Probably because the dark circles under my eyes and shuffling gait had him wondering whether I was a zombie. And then some poor schmuck handing out flyers for one of the local nightclubs got too pushy. Probably because those same dark circles under my eyes led him to mistakenly conclude I might be the sort to *frequent* nightclubs.

"Come to Club Jackrabbit tonight for mimosas and mankinis!" he told me as I shuffled past.

"Sorry, I already have plans," I muttered.

Like avoiding glittery mankinis for as long as I live.

But he didn't take the hint and tried to thrust an unwanted flyer into my hand anyway.

Strike set it on fire.

Had that been some sort of laser weapon?

Regardless, the guy backpedaled fast after that. And while I wasn't sad to see him go, I resolved to visit Zax's shop as soon as possible.

We'd told her that the person threatening me might use subtle or unusual means, and so she'd no doubt upped Strike's sensitivity settings accordingly. But this was ridiculous. Worse, I was still a hundred minutes away from being allowed to update any more of Strike's settings myself. I *really* needed an override code for that.

And yes, I knew I was focusing on the lesser problem to avoid the much more impossible ones.

I pushed through the precinct door with my hyper-sensitive drone hovering over my shoulder to find Captain Gadson waiting to introduce Aurelis and me to the team responsible for hunting down Metcalf.

The operative word being *waiting*. I was a few minutes late, and the captain was bristling with impatience.

Something Strike must have picked up on.

She surged in front of me, a small arsenal material-izing from her hull.

"Stand down! That's my boss."

"His body language is domineering. He is carrying multiple weapons. And I have been programmed to question your intelligence."

Gadson lifted an eyebrow.

"*Not* my intelligence. My orders regarding my personal protection, but that's it."

"I'm sorry, but is not the ability to rationally protect oneself a marker of intelligence?"

I sighed.

Aurelis snorted. "I like this drone. Maybe we should keep her even after the case is over."

My dragon partner showed no signs of a rough night, I noticed darkly.

I dove for Strike's power switch. "Maybe I'll turn her off until I get her back to the shop for an adjustment."

But whatever was wrong with my personal protection drone, slow reaction time wasn't one of them. She dodged out of reach.

"Strike, come here. That's an order."

"I do not have to obey your orders when your safety is at risk."

I could feel myself flushing. "My safety *isn't* at risk right now. I'm surrounded by law enforcement, and if you don't come here, I'll get them all to shoot you."

Aurelis wasn't hiding her amusement, but perhaps because Gadson was not similarly entertained, she lashed out her tail and hit the pinhead-sized switch with incredible precision.

The drone powered down, some automated process ensuring she landed safely before her propellers shut off.

I straightened and tried to look more competent than I currently felt. "Sorry, Captain. Teething problems. It won't happen again."

"No," he said. "It won't."

All right then.

He eyed me and the inert drone. "I take it you haven't had a change of heart overnight, Officer Ridley?"

"No, sir."

"Then let me introduce you to the team responsible for returning Metcalf to prison where he belongs."

The transient task force was housed three floors up and turned out to be a single scruffy-looking individual who introduced himself as Agent Fomento, head of IT.

"Where's Commander Juárez and everyone else?" Gadson barked.

"Out in the field, Captain-sir. The commander asked me to pass on his apologies."

Gadson released a breath. Slowly. "Then I suppose it's up to you to update us. What's the latest on Metcalf?"

"On who, sir?" Fomento asked with a familiar blank expression.

Cold chills raced down my spine, and Gadson and Aurelis tensed.

"Just kidding. Ha! It's a little joke we have around here."

Fomento seemed utterly oblivious to Gadson's thunderous expression. I supposed his expertise *was* with tech rather than people.

"The truth is until he cropped up to target Officer Ridley yesterday, we had almost nothing. It takes five or six days for his compulsion to wear off, so any reports of his activities we receive that way are so old as to be nearly useless, and being able to convince people to hand over their cash, buy him whatever he wants, or look the other way means it's easy for him to stay away from anything that might leave a trail. If he has a vehicle he's driving, we haven't figured out what it is. More likely he's convincing people to drive him where he wants to go and switching it up constantly. And he's done an excellent job of staying out of sight of the city surveillance network.

"Which means until yesterday, our only real hope for a lead had been for someone he's not focusing on to recognize him and call it in—that's why we've been working with the media to ask the public to report sightings—or locate him via surveillance footage. The latter is a heck of a lot easier to do if we know what city he's in and what he's after."

He nodded at me.

"We've of course been running automated facial recognition scans of the public footage readily available to us, including the photos people have been uploading to social media. But facial recognition can be thrown off with a mask or prosthetic or that sort of thing. Since yesterday though, we were able to retrace the, uh, unwilling perpetrators' steps and confirm via private surveillance footage that he approached each of them. In fact, it seems like he *wanted* us to know—after it was too late to do anything about it."

Fomento gestured to one of his many computer screens and strode over to tap his keyboard. A video showed a figure in a cowboy hat, chatting to Dylan in someone's driveway, a basketball under the kid's arm. The exchange lasted only a few seconds, and then the unknown figure turned straight toward the camera and raised the cowboy hat in a salute.

Gadson muttered something uncomplimentary under his breath.

"So with Officer Ridley, and uh, Officer Aurelis joining our team, we're feeling good about hunting him down now, sir. He's acting instead of lying low, and we know at least some of what he wants. That's why everyone's out. We caught him on surveillance, ordering breakfast from Hell's Kitchen over in Summerlin."

"Don't you think it might be a trap?" Gadson asked.

"Almost certainly. But any move we see him make is another step closer to catching him, you know? More information, more opportunity, all that. It's loads better than not even being sure if he's still in the state. And our team won't approach directly or obviously—the commander knows what he's doing."

The captain looked only mildly appeased.

"What have you learned from interviewing the apprehended cult members and Metcalf's old victims?"

"That he's a real piece of work, sir. But we already knew that."

An unwanted playback of Dr. Yanders's desperate gaze just before he'd pulled the trigger flashed through my brain. I repressed a shudder. And then a wave of guilt.

"The most interesting thing is the possibility that Metcalf helped engineer his own escape from prison," Fomento was saying.

"What do you mean?" Gadson asked. "He was supposed to be kept asleep at all times."

"He was, sir. But the Sleeping Beauty system is still relatively new and Metcalf has the most powerful mind magic to have ever been constrained by it. The doctor overseeing the prisoners had noted unusually high levels of brain activity, but since Metcalf seemed otherwise unconscious, nothing was done about it. However, when we interviewed the Order of Influence members, the empath projector who knew and worshipped Metcalf before he was incarcerated claims that Metcalf communicated with him through weak compulsions. Apparently he liked to walk past the prison sometimes just to feel close to him. And Metcalf compelled him to go and recover a set of plans he'd stashed away—plans the empath had known nothing about before then.

"It seems the cult was positioned specifically to jailbreak Metcalf out, not that they knew that. But there was this ritual where they held this golden staff thing while speaking, and that staff, after the empath replaced it with the one he'd found in the stash, compelled loyalty to Metcalf and the desire to free him every time they met. And the empath says recruiting Hale and using anti-magic to cause citywide chaos as a diversion and power tactic were Metcalf's ideas."

Gadson frowned. "Is this cult member trying to claim he was an involuntary victim?"

"No, sir. He seems quite proud of being the one Metcalf used to enact the plans."

The implications sank in with a sickening shift in my understanding. The anti-magic hostage situation that had plunged the entire city into chaos and cost multiple lives. That had threatened to kill almost every supernatural in Vegas. That had nearly killed my dad. Metcalf was behind it.

If he could engineer all that imprisoned and *in his sleep*, what on earth would he do now that he was free and fully conscious?

I remembered his words to me over the video feed. How he'd *thanked* me for helping him complete his escape.

Even if we outsmarted him a second time, what prison could hold him?

Gadson's frown deepened. "*If* that has any truth to it, do you believe he's after the iron key? And are we prepared to counter any rescue attempts Metcalf might make to free his cult members?"

I doubted we had to fear a rescue attempt. Only power and pleasure drove Metcalf. There was no sense of loyalty. No care for others. He was as selfish as only someone without empathy can be. Everyone and everything was no more than a potential tool through which to meet his desires.

So unless one of those Order of Influence members had a particular skill set Metcalf wanted, they'd rot in prison for their part in Metcalf's escape, and he wouldn't feel even the tiniest spark of guilt or remorse.

"We've temporarily installed a number of AI defensive systems around the prison and alerted Faerie officials, but no, sir. The empath didn't mention the iron key as part of Metcalf's plans. They might've come up with that part themselves. Or else it might've just been a carrot as far as Metcalf was concerned. To give the cult members additional incentive to act. This is all hypothesis, you understand. We have no proof."

No proof, and yet I didn't doubt that even imprisoned and unconscious, Metcalf's insidious power had been working for him. That even imprisoned and unconscious, he hadn't been defeated.

After all, the jailbreak scheme was a perfect demonstration of his merciless, manipulative cunning. His willingness, even eagerness, to sacrifice as many pawns necessary.

And now he was awake. Free.

And had turned the focus of that ruthless intellect on me.

I was vastly outmatched.

As if following my train of thought, Fomento looked

at me curiously. "We still have no real idea why he's so interested in Officer Ridley. He certainly can be petty and vengeful toward anyone who slights him, but not to the point of distracting him from his more ambitious goals."

I didn't know either. Not exactly. But it was clear that Metcalf had *wanted* me to find out about my past. *Wanted* me to talk to Dr. Yanders and then see him end his own life right in front of me. The trigger for the forced suicide had been my *leaving* the neurosurgeon's home, which meant Metcalf had wanted me to learn what he had to say first.

Why?

And had he anticipated I would keep that knowledge to myself?

Guilt inundated me once again. Would my withholding information be the difference between success and failure? Would it get my new teammates killed when it might have forewarned and pre-armed them?

I didn't believe this was about petty vengeance. At least not predominantly. Although it might've started out that way.

No. Metcalf had somehow found out about the history I myself had been blind to. Found out about my unusual magic. And I feared he had plans for it.

Plans that might include my magic under his command. Even though I couldn't reason *why*.

And so far, I hadn't breathed a word of this to anyone except Aurelis.

Was I making the wrong choice?

Was there any point in concealing my oddball magic abilities, or the fact I was the not-dead test subject A31438B of the Lyrebird project as Dr. Yanders had advised, when Metcalf and his designs on me likely included no such reservation?

My life, my career, my understanding of who I was, was slipping through my fingers, and I wanted to get off this carnival ride from hell.

But I knew it was only just beginning.

Metcalf had barely scratched the surface of what he was capable of.

Aurelis gave me a hard stare and ever so slightly shook her head.

So I kept my silence and surrendered any hope of peace until Metcalf was caught... or I was dead.

CHAPTER THIRTEEN

The task force commander hadn't left any orders for us with Fomento, so I visited briefly with Stewie to make sure he knew he'd be released on bail in four more days —as soon as we could be certain any remaining compulsions had worn off. I also ordered him and Zeus fancy burgers for brunch, promised to get him some books and doggy enrichment games to pass the time, and decided to dash out to get Strike's settings adjusted while I had the chance.

Aurelis dragged her gaze reluctantly from her book when I told her where I was going. "Need an escort?"

She sounded like she'd rather acquire a scale mite infestation.

"Nah." The day was a scorcher, my head and body ached with fatigue, and I didn't feel like walking. Especially with my hypersensitive drone threatening to shoot everyone around me. "I'll splurge and catch a cab straight there and straight back and not leave Zax's shop in between."

My partner gave me a sour look. "And you'll have your drone on the entire time. Even inside the cab."

"Yes, ma'am."

I phoned a cab, lugged Strike's dead weight down to the ground floor and outside, and paused to locate her power button.

A taxi pulled up to the curb. That was fast. I glanced up to let them know I'd be a second. But one of the heavily tinted rear windows rolled down an inch, and a man's voice drifted out.

"Leave the drone powered off and get in without drawing attention, Lyra. You and I should have a chat."

I knew that voice. Calm and authoritative with an edge of charm. Metcalf might've come from a backwater town, but he didn't talk like it. Yet it wasn't his words that bent me to his will.

No. Getting this close and speaking aloud was merely for effect.

Beneath the power play, his magic was terrifyingly real. Cold and hard and unyielding as a vise.

I tucked Strike back under my arm and got in the cab.

The taxi driver did not turn around or even look at me in the rearview mirror. I knew there would be no help from him.

Hell, if he was a real cabbie, he might not even suspect anything was wrong.

A woman I didn't recognize sat in the front passenger seat. Even in profile, her beauty was striking. Her jawline curved gracefully down to her pointed chin, highlighting her flawless skin and the echoing sweep of her cheekbones. Her lips were full, eyelashes a thick fringe around light green eyes, and her tumble of dark honey curls was like something out of a magic-enhanced shampoo commercial.

For a moment, I feared that Metcalf had chosen her because of that beauty, that he'd forced her to—

No.

Nothing I'd read mentioned him indulging in that particular perversion. Metcalf had likely brought her along as either a hostage or because she could protect him in some other form. Probably by way of her magic, although I spotted a sheath for a short, bladed weapon strapped to her thigh.

I committed what I could see of her to memory, hoping that knowing what she looked like might become useful somewhere down the track. That there'd even *be* a somewhere down the track.

Then she tucked her commercial-worthy hair behind her ear. Her pointed ear. And goose bumps prickled along my arms in a way that had nothing to do with the air-conditioning.

A fae. Without wings, even invisible ones, so far as I could tell, but definitely a fae.

Whose glamour meant Metcalf could look like whomever he wanted to. And whose versatile, if limited, magic could do untold damage under his callous command.

The perfect accessory for a criminal fugitive wanting to move freely through a city full of people who'd love nothing more than to turn him in.

No wonder the team hunting him hadn't been able to pin down even his general location until now.

How had Metcalf managed to overwhelm the fae's substantial magical defenses? He must have caught her on some external duty. I refused to believe he was powerful enough to walk into Faerie and take what he wanted.

But *she* probably could.

Would his compulsions wear off if she returned to Faerie? Was my family even still safe?

I swallowed hard and turned my attention unwillingly to the devil himself.

He sat in the back on the opposite side of the cab. Far, far too close for comfort. Watching me. Controlling me. Not bothering to appear in any likeness but his own before me.

When it came to kidnapping or hostage situations, that was never a good sign.

Unlike his fae captive, Metcalf's physical presence was unremarkable. There was a touch of color to his pasty skin that hadn't been there when I'd last seen him —a benefit of recent sun after three years in a blackout prison. Two weeks of freedom had treated him well. But his frame was still scrawny, his round face nondescript. It was the calculation in his eyes and the horror of his magic pressing against my own will that made his presence a crushing weight within the confines of the car. Made me want to shrink away like that might protect me.

He was utterly calm, despite being right outside a building brimming with law enforcement personnel who were hunting him even now. As a true psychopath, his heart would not be thudding in his ears, his breathing would remain steady, and his sympathetic nervous system wouldn't dump a load of adrenaline into his system. No, his pulse wouldn't even be elevated— except perhaps in pleasurable anticipation of this power trip.

He did not feel stress. Did not fear society's judgment or any punishment we could mete out. Nor did he feel the least amount of empathy.

I knew there was no point pleading for mercy he did not possess.

He smiled. A charming yet empty curve of his lips that made my gut tighten.

"Hello, Lyra. I'm so glad we could finally meet."

Such a simple phrase. The implications of it made

me want to throw myself out the moving vehicle.

Based on my pounding heart and limbs trembling with chemical readiness, *my* acute stress response was working just fine. But I didn't move. *Couldn't* move.

"Go to hell," I spat. But the words came out weaker than I'd like.

Metcalf ignored me and nodded at Strike. "The drone was a clever idea," he said like he was praising a toddler. "But utterly useless now I'm aware of it."

I opened my mouth and shut it again. What on earth could I say to this man that would have any effect?

He didn't force me to speak. Not yet.

And I felt nauseatingly grateful for the temporary reprieve. Because I very much needed the chance to pull myself together.

The cab sighed to a stop mere minutes after picking me up. We were outside my apartment building.

I should've been trying to anticipate what was coming. If there was any trick I could use or opportunity I could exploit to escape. To draw attention. Anything. But all I could think about was how glad I was that my family wasn't home.

I was so grateful they were in the relative safety of Faerie I could've cried.

We left the cabbie behind, Metcalf's features changing beyond recognition before we exited, and the three of us, the fae woman, the devil, and I, walked up to my apartment.

We didn't hurry. There was no need. And that, more

than anything else Metcalf had done so far, drove home just how helpless I was.

We shared the elevator with one of my neighbors, and I made polite small talk about the weather and his new magitech toaster. Then we were in my apartment and Metcalf's glamoured visage fell away.

"Aren't you going to show me some hospitality?"

He phrased it as a question, but his magic allowed no such leeway.

"Can I get you a drink?" I asked. "Coffee? Soda? Beer? Tea?"

"A green tea would be lovely, thank you."

I wrinkled my nose. I only kept green tea on hand for my brother Dimitri, who was fond of it. Personally I was a black coffee kind of girl—or hot chocolate if I wanted to splurge. But I switched on the kettle and dug the box of jasmine tea out from the back of the cupboard, then rummaged for a second clean mug.

Okay, I wasn't a great hostess even for guests I *wanted* in my apartment.

Metcalf let me work in silence like he had all the time in the world. Like he didn't have federal and local law enforcement searching for him this very moment. Like I posed no threat to him at all... Which, to my disgust, was probably true.

The human psyche could house two conflicting desires. It happened all the time. The desire to lose weight and the desire to eat that piece of cake. The desire to provide for your family and the desire to tell your boss to shove it. The desire to be a loving partner and the desire to win an argument. We could also want a single thing and act in direct contradiction to that want. The addict who wants to quit. The loving parent who snaps at their child. The person who wants something so badly that the fear of failing makes them self-sabotage before they can start to hope.

Being under Metcalf's control was like both those things, except worse. His magic placed a compulsion so strong it overrode your conflicting desires, but it didn't over*write* them. They were still there. Screaming at you to stop.

At least he couldn't overwrite them the first time. But enough months under his brainwashing magic and the existing neural pathways in your brain grew weaker and weaker. Until you lost yourself. Until you acted like and actually *were* a loyal fanatic.

As I waited for the water to heat, my mind fantasized about escaping. About using the phone in my pocket to surreptitiously alert the team Metcalf was in my apartment. About throwing the boiling water over his unprotected face and taking him down while he screamed. But my shaking hand poured the water into the mugs instead. Because more than any of those things, I wanted to serve him tea.

I carried the two mugs over to the coffee table by the couch and placed his in front of him. Then, against every part of my better judgment, I sat down.

Metcalf nursed the cup between his palms but pinned his eyes on me.

"I have plans for you, my little lyrebird."

Lyrebird. The word jolted me like an electric shock.

Once again, I saw Dr. Yanders lifting the gun to his temple. The red and pink spatter over the couch and carpet.

Metcalf took a languid sip of the tea my traitorous hands had made him. "I won't spoil the surprise by telling you what they are just yet. But rest assured, you feature heavily in them. That's why I had to put you through your paces yesterday."

Outwardly, I didn't respond. But inside, dread dragged at me like a sodden and heavy fishing net. Trying to pull me under.

"Did you know the more times I plant compulsions within you, the less defenses you hold? Like a cliff crumbling under the weight of the sea, your mind becomes more and more malleable beneath my power."

He watched me, wanting to see my reaction. The fear, the horror, the helplessness. So I shoved it down deep and didn't give him the pleasure.

"You talk tough for someone I could take down easily in a fair fight," I pointed out.

"Fair? Life isn't fair, little lyrebird. Fair is just an empty construct society attempts to manipulate us with. I'm surprised you haven't figured that out yet." He paused and took another sip of his tea.

There was no point in talking, I reminded myself.

My words held no more weight to him than a cockroach's plea to the boot about to step on it. I was only drawing out his amusement.

Was there any point in doing that? Would Aurelis come looking for me if I could drag it out long enough?

"Come and get a taste of my power," Metcalf ordered.

My body snapped to obey before my mind finished processing what he'd said. I reached for his wrist and felt the unpleasant heady sensation of his magic flow through me.

I recoiled. Too late. "Why would you give me your magic?"

He chuckled. "You still haven't figured it out? You're a *mimic*, Lyra. So I don't need to give you anything. Quite the opposite, in fact. With you under my control, my power is effectively doubled."

Of course. *Lyrebird.* It was right there in the name.

I felt like an idiot. This self-obsessed maniac had figured out more about my past and my magic in a week or two than I had in my twenty-two years.

And now I was his to use.

"What does it feel like when you mimic someone's power?" he asked. "Describe it to me."

I tried to explain. How I could *feel* the shape, the unique signature or essence of someone's magic whenever we touched. How some magics felt friendly or soothing, others alluring, and others sharp and dangerous. How some felt simple and straightforward and others unfathomably complex. Except it was something instinctive, something I sensed on a deep subconscious level that could not be easily transcribed into words.

"And what happens when you lose contact?"

I supposed what I'd always assumed was me drawing some of their power into myself must have actually been my magic reshaping itself to match theirs. And without continued contact, without the continued input of that unique signature, of what the magic should feel like, my power forgot what it was supposed to be mimicking and gradually fell out of sync.

Metcalf stood up. "Give mine a try." He forced me to move to the window with him and draw on—no, *mirror*—his magic again. "Look down at the pedestrians walking below. Heedless of your existence. See the man in the red shirt? Compel him to walk into that concrete wall."

Acutely cognizant of the horror of being a victim of Metcalf's magic, I used that same magic against the man in the red shirt.

He walked so unhesitatingly into the wall that when he reeled back, even three floors up I could see the blood gushing from his nose.

My cheeks burned with shame.

Metcalf chuckled beside me. "Fun, isn't it? But that's child's play. I have my sights set on something far more... sophisticated."

"You're insane."

"Not at all. I see what I want, and I go after it. Few people are more perfectly clearheaded than that."

I tried to use his own magic against him. But of course, he'd ensured I was thoroughly under his control before giving it to me. All my limbs were suffering from the same misguided loyalty. The only thing that was still mine was my tongue.

"What do you want from me?" I ground out. Maybe if he told me, I could figure out a way to stop it somehow.

"Today? Nothing. Go on about your life as usual. Your connections or access may prove useful at some point, and this way your colleagues can keep sniffing up the wrong tree. You will tell no one. Hint at nothing. And do everything in your power to avoid raising suspicion." He patted me on the head. "Until next time…"

It wasn't a threat. It was a promise.

My teeth clenched so hard I started to worry about dental bills.

"Oh, and by the way, convince your drone I'm your friendly uncle. No. Your boss's boss. Yes, I like that. Means I can order you around."

He strolled to the door and gave me that first charming smile again.

"See you later, alligator."

The stupid phrase had never been so sinister.

CHAPTER FOURTEEN

I powered Strike on. Not that she'd do me much good now, of course.

"I can't protect you if you keep turning me off!" she complained.

She had no idea how right she was. Not that it would've taken Metcalf long to find a way around her anyway. I'd been stupid to think a single drone—no matter how suspicious—could keep me safe from a psychopath with more power than anyone should possess. If it came to it, he'd have no qualms about conscripting an army of people off the street to take her down. As many as it took and who cared about the casualties.

"Sorry," I mumbled. "But you can't threaten to attack anyone who looks at me funny either."

She hovered closer. "Are you having a bad day again? Your body language appears downcast. But you're not eating sugar-laden ice cream."

I rubbed my face. "Do I get a gold star for effort?"

"If you require encouragement from an artificial intelligence programmed to parrot uplifting phrases, you should have chosen an emotional support drone."

I wondered if Zax had modeled Strike's interpersonal skills on Aurelis.

I also wondered if, since Strike was about to be rendered almost entirely useless to me, whether I could skip the trip to Zax's shop.

"Good tip. Speaking of tips, has it been a thousand minutes since I last updated your settings yet?"

"Yes."

"Good. Let's create a new rule of thumb then."

"I don't have a thumb."

"It's an expression that means—"

"I know what it means. I just looked it up. But it's a poor word choice substitute for protocol."

"How come your skills extend to correcting my use of language but not offering encouragement?"

"I am awaiting new protocol instructions."

"Right. Your new protocol is that you are only to intervene if someone trains a weapon on me or physically assaults me. You will not take any action beyond observation until one of those things happens."

"But by then it may be too late for a successful intervention."

"It's a calculated risk that I'm willing to take."

My logic was twofold. One, with the magical

advances of modern medicine, most injuries were survivable. Two, I'd already met with the bastard I'd acquired Strike to protect me from—and now I had the uncomfortable impression his plans for me didn't involve my death.

Not yet anyway. And I wondered if death might be preferable.

"This is non-negotiable," I stated firmly. "Otherwise I'm returning you to Zax."

She hummed over that for a minute. "Setting—"

"Wait. Just to clarify, you may also intervene if"—I swallowed, remembering the bloody remains of Dr. Yanders's head again—"if I turn a weapon on myself."

"Setting updated," she chirped. "But perhaps you should reconsider an emotional support drone."

I sighed. "There's one last thing. After your mishap with my captain today, I want to ensure you'll recognize my other bosses." I brought up two photos on my phone. "This is Commander Juárez in charge of my current task force assignment. And this is my boss's boss."

"According to my facial recognition software and a crosscheck of LVMPD records, your boss's boss is Colton Metcalf. A wanted criminal."

My eyes widened. "How do you have access to LVMPD records?" Not that she needed them. Metcalf's face was all over the news.

"That information is proprietary," Strike told me.

I wondered if proprietary was code for illegal. But

really, I had bigger problems. How was I supposed to explain this?

As much as most of me would've liked to fail at the first task Metcalf had given me—well, second if you counted forcing that stranger to smash himself into a wall—my brain helpfully offered up a solution.

"That information is above your security clearance. So you'll just have to take my word for it and *not* attack him on sight."

"But my programmer highlighted Metcalf as the most probable threat."

"I can't comment on the details of the case. But the new protocol still stands."

Strike's propellers whirred faster in a distinctly whiny tone.

"I know humans are frequently irrational, but you make even less sense than most."

I snorted. "How would you know? Isn't this your first assignment?"

"I am able to extrapolate from general data," she informed me. Snootily, I thought, but maybe that was just my imagination.

I didn't want to return to the precinct. Well, the part of me that Metcalf *hadn't* meddled with didn't want to return to the precinct. In the space of ten minutes, I'd gone from being an asset in my new task force to a liability to everyone I worked with.

A traitorous—potentially lethal—liability.

How could I get anywhere near my friends and coworkers now that Metcalf had wormed his way into my brain?

I'd seen what his power could do. Seen how unerringly Stewie had leveled the submachine gun at the innocent pedestrians below. How a scared kid I'd never met pushed me to my intended death. And I'd felt the viselike grip of Metcalf's magic on my own mind.

I was under no illusion that if he compelled me to kill someone—anyone—that I'd be able to do anything except obey.

My jaw ached from clenching my teeth, and my stomach was knotted so tight even a sailor wouldn't be able to undo it.

I should've taken Gadson up on his offer of a safe house. I should've never turned Strike off.

Yet recriminations were useless. If Metcalf had decided he wanted me for whatever evil scheme he was concocting, then nothing I could've done would've been sufficient.

I wasn't made for subterfuge. Concealing things from people I cared about was like a scab I couldn't stop poking.

I massaged the muscles of my jaw. The Metcalf part of my brain was ordering me to calm down. To find a way to soothe myself. Because I had to do everything in my power to avoid raising suspicion.

There were two details I could focus on and find comfort in. One, so far, Metcalf hadn't compelled me to harm or act against anyone at my precinct.

Not that I was aware of anyway.

Could he plant a compulsion in me without my knowledge until the time came to act?

I didn't know.

Pain radiated from my clenched teeth.

Okay. So there was *one* detail I found comfort in.

My family was protected in Faerie. And Metcalf hadn't even made mention of them. That was good, right? I got the sense his focus was elsewhere—that he had bigger plans. Plans more important to him than torturing me.

And Aurelis was damn hard to kill. If I was ordered to shoot her point-blank, she'd gulp me down in a couple of bites and use the gun to pick my remains out of her teeth.

There was some comfort in that too.

I phoned Miles as Strike and I caught a cab back to the precinct. Both parts of my brain liked that idea. *I* wanted to hear my father's voice. Reassure myself they were safe. Rest for a few moments in the relief of having achieved that much at least. And the traitorous part of my brain figured it was part of maintaining my normal facade and might make me less of a nervous wreck to boot.

I drew in a few steadying breaths while I waited for him to pick up.

"Darling, I was wondering when you'd call."

"Hey, Dad." My voice came out strangled by the tension in my throat, and I coughed to clear it. "How have you settled in?"

"Good. The kids are having a ball."

"What about you?"

"I haven't left the property much, but when I have, no fae has done worse than give me a dirty look." He sounded genuinely baffled. "Ronan's family name must carry a lot of weight around here."

Did it now? Ronan never had explained exactly where he fit within Faerie society. Did all fae have a lord or lady prefix to their names? Or did he have more reason than most to dislike politics and power games?

"All right. What's the story with vampires and fae anyway?"

"Ah." Miles sounded uncomfortable. "The fae are particularly susceptible to a vampire's bite. All we need to do is nick a vein, and they're immobilized until we're done. And if we drink fae blood, some of their immense power is temporarily passed onto us. So there was a time—"

I put him out of his misery. "Yeah, okay. I get the picture."

Wow. Ronan had really put his neck on the line for me then.

Hmm. Perhaps that was a poor turn of phrase.

But I remembered his evasion when I'd asked what it had cost him. I'd thought it was bad enough that he'd elected to take on my family as his personal houseguests. Now I understood he was risking far more than inconvenience and broken crockery.

I swallowed down my guilt. Because what other choice was there?

"How does Ronan seem to be coping with the troublemakers?"

"Well, it's a bit of a squeeze to fit us all in his house. Imagine a splendid log cabin crossed with a tree house for grown-ups and you'll get some idea of what it's like. But it's deep in the forest, and his property is large enough that we don't see him much. The kids adore it. Although Ronan's parents keep inviting themselves over for dinner, and then all three of them become as formal and unbending as planks of wood. And his parents keep asking questions about you."

Huh? "What sorts of questions?"

"Strange questions. Like your health history. Your favorite flowers. Your political views. Whether you've ever been married or borne children or—"

The list was making me increasingly uncomfortable, so I cut him off. "Maybe they don't realize Ronan is simply repaying a favor."

Miles was unconvinced. "Maybe. But if so, Ronan hasn't bothered to correct them. What were your feelings toward *him* again?"

Time to move the conversation along.

"So, what's Faerie like anyway?"

"I understood you were here recently."

"Sure, but I only saw border security and the inside of a prison cell."

"Well then, you'd best come visit us and find out for yourself," he said cheerfully.

And just like that, the tenuous bubble of normalcy and warmth I'd built up imploded. Tears pricked at the corners of my vision. There was nothing I'd rather do than take him up on his offer. But I couldn't. Not when I couldn't trust myself.

There was no way to explain that to my overly astute father. So I bit my cheek until I was sure my voice wouldn't give me away and said, "Can't wait."

CHAPTER FIFTEEN

Metcalf was ruining my life.

I'd expected things to get worse ever since the rooftop incident. But this was a misery I hadn't anticipated.

Cars crawled through the busy intersection, their occupants glowering at me like this was *my* idea of a good time. The older vehicles spewed hot, noxious fumes as they grumbled past, and even the newer models added to the already unpleasant heat trap of asphalt baking under the desert sun.

Sweat made my hair cling needily to the back of my neck, and more of it was trickling down my spine. I was wearing an LVMPD-issued hat and sunglasses, but neither helped overly much.

The task force commander's bright idea to capture Metcalf?

Traffic duty.

His logic was sound enough—based on the information he had. My normal duties were too unpredictable for the good guys to anticipate and too easy for Metcalf to manipulate. If I was going to play bait, Commander Juárez needed me in a role where I'd stay in the same place for long hours. That way the task force could have an anti-magic field set up and ready to activate, a perimeter watch in position before my arrival, and a huge team of hand-selected law enforcement personnel and attack drones ready to rush in at a moment's notice.

Hence, traffic duty.

I might've felt less bitter about it if I hadn't known Metcalf wouldn't come for me. Hadn't known he'd already made his move and wasn't even playing on the same game board anymore.

But seriously, couldn't Juárez have come up with a post that included air-conditioning? If I was going to be dangled as bait, it would've been nice to be *climate-controlled* bait.

Down here between the rows upon rows of buildings, there were none of the cooling breezes I enjoyed on Aurelis's back. And speaking of my partner, *she* was standing on the sidewalk "supervising" because her majestic size in the middle of the intersection only added to the traffic congestion.

The truth of that did not mitigate my feelings of peevish resentment.

At least Strike was hovering next to me in solidarity. Hopefully spending all day in the full sun wouldn't overheat her circuits. On the downside, that meant she was close enough to ask questions.

Whose idea had it been to equip drivers with car horns? Didn't the human race have more advanced methods of communicating? Did I know my skin was red and sticky-looking? Why was I performing a repetitive task better suited to a machine? Why did I choose to do so many things that made me unhappy? Why was I glaring at her like that?

I flipped the sign around and made the hand gestures for anyone the sign was too subtle for. Then I squirted some of the lukewarm water from my drink bottle into my mouth.

Word was that I shouldn't expect this set of traffic lights to be repaired for at least several days.

Strike asked me another question.

I let out a heavy sigh and wondered what her protocols said about protecting herself from me.

I trudged up to my apartment simultaneously relieved and apprehensive that my workday was over. The worst thing about traffic control was that the duties were so mind-numbingly boring that there was nothing to keep my mind off Metcalf.

What was he planning? Would he be waiting for me when I got home? Why was he so interested in me and my magic? What terrible thing would he force me to do next? And how many would die before this was over?

The neurosurgeon's death had been reported as a suicide, the story picked up by only a few local news outlets. Of course, Aurelis and I knew better. But we hadn't told anyone, and that chafed at me like I'd rolled around in a patch of desert thistles and hadn't extracted the spines yet.

Strike did a lap of the apartment and then went straight to her charging station.

I went straight to the shower, grumbling about how unfair it was that drones and dragons didn't need to sweat.

Still, as much as I was envious of Aurelis in her supervisory role and her love of basking in the sun, the truth was that by the end of the day, she'd looked less than impressed by our new assignment. I figured she hadn't joined the Metcalf task force expecting to be bored stupid.

But that was the one *upside* to traffic control as well. There was almost no interaction with my colleagues, which made it far easier to hide the fact I was a nervous wreck and avoid raising suspicion.

I told myself it might make it harder for Metcalf to use me against them as well. But myself was highly skeptical.

Lucky for me, my stomach decided it couldn't subsist on tension alone and let out a growl loud enough to derail my train of thought.

So when I stepped out of the shower, I was wondering where to order takeout from now that Vargas had rolled his tank through my favorite option. Screw Metcalf anyway.

That was when Strike thudded against the bathroom door.

"Your boss's boss just parked in front of the building."

Every pleasant clean sensation the shower had given me shriveled and died. I threw on clothes without toweling off first. No way did I want Metcalf walking in on me half-naked.

My undies twisted awkwardly as I dragged them up, and it took three tries for my trembling fingers to hook the clasp on my bra.

Since I hadn't brought a clean outfit into the shower with me, my only options were the sweaty police uniform I'd just discarded, the cutesy sloth summer pajamas I'd been planning on changing into, or a pair of running shorts and tank top that hadn't made it into my laundry hamper yet.

I opted for the latter, yanked them on, and manhandled my wet hair into a ponytail so it was out of my face. It dripped down my back much like the sweat had, only colder and more prolific.

Then I was filled with the overwhelming urge to open the front door. I dropped the trainer I'd been about to pull on and rushed over to do it.

The hallway was empty.

Another urge drove me backward a few steps, and I shut and relocked the door.

Metcalf materialized in my living room.

I would've shrieked if my lungs had been my own.

The bastard liked whatever he saw on my face. "Fae glamour is rather useful, isn't it? There are so few limits when you can commandeer others' magic for your own."

Beside him, a second figure materialized more slowly. The beautiful honey-blond woman who'd been in the front of the cab. But she stood stiff and silent, and Metcalf's attention was solely on me.

"You of all people would have at least some idea of what I'm talking about, wouldn't you, little lyrebird?"

It wasn't really a question.

"What do you want with me, you cowardly piece of shit?" I snapped.

The outburst probably had more to do with exhaustion than bravery.

The woman's expression flickered. I wasn't sure if the fleeting curve of her lips had been a smile or a grimace.

Still, I didn't need to see her statued form to know it was hopeless. But I'd had enough of taking whatever Metcalf threw at me without a fight.

It was a dumb move.

My own hand rose and slapped me across the cheek. Once. Twice. Three times.

Metcalf smirked. "Oh dear. Please refrain from hitting yourself."

Strike hovered next to me, apparently uncertain whether an open hand counted as a weapon according to her new settings. "Is this part of the thing that's above my security clearance?"

My head jerked in a nod even as my hand struck my cheek again. Tears of equal parts rage and humiliation sprang to my eyes, but I refused to give Metcalf the satisfaction of letting them fall.

He waved his own hand as if growing tired of the game.

"Now, my little protégé, it's time to get serious about your training."

Protégé?

"Training for what?" I ground out when he stared at me expectantly.

"To be my very own personal assistant. It can get tiresome maintaining control over every insect I've caught in my web, and it gets in the way of me pursuing more interesting pursuits. But you can use my magic. You can even use magic I don't possess. It's quite impressive really. Everyone wants to be special, but so few are…"

His gaze had grown distant as he'd spoken, but now it jerked back to me. "If I wasn't so confident that I could mold you into the perfect loyal servant, I'd have to kill you instead."

Well. At least my takeout dilemma was solved.

I'd lost my appetite.

What the heck was he thinking? Was he expecting me to follow him around, holding his hand to mimic his magic and do all his dirty work?

"But that's the long-term plan since your complete conversion will take months," Metcalf added. "Before that, I will show the world what I'm capable of. An appropriate way to celebrate my regained freedom, don't you think? And you're going to help me."

He stepped in close and caressed my stinging cheek, his voice lowering to an intimate whisper.

"Spoiler alert. I'm going to lay waste to Washington, DC. But no one will even care what happened to Washington by the time we're through."

I wanted to scream. To tell Strike to shoot him down, or make myself grab the coffee table and slam it over his stupid skull. But—of course—I did none of those things.

And Strike didn't intervene on her own initiative, because I'd ordered her not to. Ordered her to do nothing but observe unless specific conditions were met.

I had no idea what she was making of this conversation, but since she found humans highly illogical, perhaps this was no more puzzling to her than eating ice cream.

My fellow prisoner did not react either.

Metcalf slipped something from his pocket.

A sentiment stone. Like the one I'd bought for Miles's birthday, only nicer. The waxy seal was still in place, which meant it was unused.

Dread followed closely on the heels of my confusion. I'd never thought of the sentiment stone as a weapon before. Yet in the hands of Metcalf, its abilities took on a sinister light. Would he force me to do something horrifying and capture every gut-wrenching sensation of it in the stone just so he could force me to relive it over and over again? Or was it something else? Something worse? What if he'd figured out how to shortcut the process of turning me permanently into his dutiful puppet?

I swallowed down bile.

"I see you know what this is," Metcalf observed. "Good. Take it."

My hand obeyed, wrapping around the smooth, warm stone.

Metcalf slid several compulsions at me at once, his amusement in toying with me shifting to something more businesslike. Quieter, but not at all safer. Like a predator fixating on their prey.

"You know what to do."

I removed the seal on the stone, and Metcalf held out his hand. I took that too. Then focused on the unpleasant heady sweetness of his magic, my own magic automatically shifting to match until I was flooded with the same evil power. And all the while, I poured every detail of the experience into the sentiment stone.

Metcalf watched me intently as I released my grip on both his hand and the stone. As I waited for my magic to lose the shape of his, the way it had done for any magic I'd "borrowed" throughout my life. And once it was gone, he watched me reclaim the sentiment stone.

The sense of his magic hit me as clearly as if I was

gripping his wrist instead of the stone. And my magic mimicked it. His power swelling inside me.

Holy craps table.

Metcalf had figured out how to circumvent my magic's need for contact. At least as long as the stone lasted.

It was a breakthrough I would've paid through the nose for many a time over the course of my life. From my first magic show-and-tell in middle school, to every time I'd been teased or criticized for having no real magic of my own—or reprimanded or suspended for "stealing" someone else's.

And all it had taken was one ludicrously expensive sentiment stone.

Well, that and the understanding that my magic *mimicked* others. Not siphoned it. Something I'd been clueless to until yesterday.

But any reflexive spark of excitement bled from me as fast as it had risen.

The self-named devil wanted me to be his personal assistant. To help "show the world what he was capable of" in some catastrophic event that would leave Washington in ruin—and that tragedy not even noteworthy in the greater horror to come.

And now he had an independent puppet. A puppet with access to the LVMPD and all that entailed. A puppet who should not—but would—possess a perfect copy of Metcalf's insidious manipulative power.

A puppet no one would suspect until it was too late.

The puppet master jerked my strings. I turned to the fae woman and slid a tendril of magic into her. More magic than I'd needed on the human I'd shoved into the wall, but it was still too easy.

She slapped herself across the cheek. Hard enough to leave a red handprint on her flawless skin. And I watched her eyes widen in shock, then narrow in humiliation and helplessness and hatred. Everything I'd been feeling only moments before... Except this time those feelings were directed at me.

I ran to the bathroom and vomited. Metcalf's hold on my mind apparently decided that letting me puke elsewhere was in his best interest.

And then my psychopathic dictator gave me my new orders.

CHAPTER SIXTEEN

The jostling crowd smelled of body odor, alcohol, and the faint metallic tang of blood. The standing-room-only area around the fight cage was the worst, so I skirted around it until I was below one of the suspended walkways opponents used to enter the cage. Then I found a spot in the grandstand. I was pretty sure that was close enough.

Bookies lined the outer walls except for where two long bars stretched on opposite sides. Some of those bookies even still accepted paper money. One of them would be my next stop. But the fighters due to come on in a minute were too evenly matched. The odds not high enough.

I'd only been here once before. On a date I should never have agreed to. Gratuitous violence and bloodshed weren't really my scene, and I wasn't pleased to be back.

The couple I was lurking next to didn't share my

views. Dissecting the upcoming fight with as much enthusiasm as Blake dissected the discoveries of ancient tombs that shed light on the lives of sapient peoples long dead. I tuned them out, brushing the lump in my pocket for the hundredth time and cursing Metcalf and his stupid assignment.

The announcer's voice boomed through the cavernous space as two shifters in human form emerged at opposite ends of the stadium and started down the suspended walkways.

After the supernaturals revealed themselves, shifter matches quickly became MMA fan favorites. Shifters' strength, speed, and incredible ability to heal meant the matches were brutal, proficient, and bloody.

The crowd went wild, cheering and whistling and screaming like they were determined to cause hearing damage to everyone around them. I had no idea how shifters and other supernaturals with heightened senses could stand it.

The mission Metcalf had given me was simple. Rig one of the fights. Make loads of money. And use that money to buy more sentiment stones.

All it required was illicit magic use and possibly ruining someone's career.

I might not agree with the fights, but that didn't mean I wanted to stop the people who loved them from participating.

The shifters made it to the arena and proceeded to beat each other bloody. They stayed in human form and fought without any weapons besides their own bodies, but that only made the fight more vicious.

Huge screens suspended from the ceiling replayed the moments of contact at speeds the human eye could actually track. Flesh and bone caved, blood sprayed, and distressing cries of agony were dragged from the fighter's throats. Shifters could heal almost anything at crazily swift speeds, but it didn't stop them from feeling pain.

The crowd loved it.

I wanted to leave. Right now. And watch *My Little Pegasus* reruns with Sage or something.

But Metcalf had given me a mission, and I couldn't get out of here until I'd completed it.

As the odds suggested, the fighters were evenly matched, which meant each round lasted the full five violent minutes. I was thoroughly sick of it by then. But up next was the wild card match—where an unknown or long-shot contender would face an established champion for a chance at glory.

This was the one I'd been waiting for.

I threaded my way through all the people likewise heading toward the bookies or the bar. I needed to lay my bet fast enough to get back to my spot under the walkway before the champion came out. I wasn't sure how long I had. The next match time was clear, but who knew how long they'd give the fighter beforehand to rev up the crowd.

I plonked down the stack of cash Metcalf had given

me onto the counter. "All of this on the underdog to win by submission."

The bookie didn't bat an eyelid. "Sure. Here's your ticket."

I elbowed my way back to the grandstand. Trying not to think about what Metcalf would do to me if the champion was knocked out instead.

Or what the fans might do to me if it worked perfectly, the favorite reported someone had meddled with his brain, and they linked that to me as the biggest winner.

Should I try to be subtle? Or outright compel him to lose? To submit.

My stomach knotted in discomfort. But things could be a lot worse. The fighter would recover from whatever I did tonight.

Wouldn't he?

I shut my eyes. If I was honest with myself, I knew chances were I'd commit far more terrible acts before Metcalf was through with me.

If he would *ever* be through with me.

And I had no choice in the matter anyway. So there was no point giving myself a stomach ulcer over it.

Or was that the Metcalf parasite in my brain trying to brush away the *wrongness* of what I was about to do—to keep its host in better shape?

The announcer's voice reverberated around the stadium again with a five-minute warning, and the laggards rushed back to their spots, spilling drinks and spouting predictions. Few seemed to be betting on the underdog.

Then the huge muscular champion was striding down the walkway above me, and the crowd roared their deafening approval.

I shoved my hand into my pocket to grip the smooth warmth of the sentiment stone. Metcalf's ugly magic thrummed within me, and I sent it toward the shifter champion.

Now was not the time for subtlety, I decided. I didn't have the skill with Metcalf's magic or the intimate knowledge of the MMA to try gentle nudges throughout the fight. *Let the underdog win,* I willed him. *Make it believable. Rough him up. But let him win by submission in the end.*

The huge man's stride hitched for half a second, but then he continued down the walkway.

Tell no one, I rushed to add, *ever.*

It wouldn't stop him forever. The compulsion would fade over time. But it was as good as I could do. Besides, the guy probably deserved to tell someone what happened someday. Who knew whether anyone would believe him?

Hell, who knew if Las Vegas would even exist by then? I didn't know what Metcalf was planning, but it was clear obliterating Washington, DC, was only the beginning.

My throat thickened, and I wished I'd thought to get

a drink from the bar. Water maybe. Or something stronger.

The fight commenced. I forced myself to watch every blow the champion took under my compulsion. Every grunt. Every spray of blood. Every broken bone.

My inexperienced eye couldn't tell much about his opponent, but I thought from the crowd's reaction they were shocked by how things were panning out.

I really hoped the favorite wouldn't be accused of throwing the match. That would be far more ruinous to his career than a surprise one-off blemish on his otherwise impressive record.

The underdog seemed to grow more confident as the rounds progressed. His blows becoming harder, surer, faster. But if he didn't do something big and bad soon, the guy I'd compelled was going to have a hard time making a submission believable.

Finally the challenger locked the champion's head in a savage choke hold. The compelled man made a show of fighting while his face turned red, more red, and tinged toward purple. I unconsciously held my breath along with him. Then he submitted the match with a hand that wouldn't have still worked if he'd been human.

Feeling sick with revulsion yet again, I left the grandstand to cash in my ticket.

CHAPTER SEVENTEEN

The sunshine streaming cheerfully through my bedroom window seemed all wrong. There was nothing I was looking forward to about today. And an awful lot that I wasn't.

I groaned as last night's events trickled back to me. The revelation of the sentiment stone. The second revelation of how useful that made me under Metcalf's control.

Forcing the fae to slap herself and the humiliation and hatred I'd seen in her gaze. Forcing the fighter to take painful blow after painful blow and lose his winning streak to a wild card opponent. Taking the almost year's salary worth of winnings to four different shops to acquire five sentiment stones and prevent the sellers from questioning why on earth anyone would need so many.

Trudging home with the sentiment stones burning holes in my pockets, then remembering I hadn't eaten and had very little food in the house. Showering again. Like it could wash away the dirtiness I felt clinging to me, only to realize it wasn't my skin that felt dirty. Almost falling asleep standing up while I nuked a bowl of canned soup in the microwave and forced myself to swallow it down despite the nausea.

And then nothing... until the stupid cheerful sunshine.

I checked the time. One minute before my alarm.

I groaned again. One minute wasn't nearly enough time to wallow in self-pity.

My phone blared with the chiming tone I'd found appealing when I'd selected it a year ago. Not anymore. I narrowly overcame the urge to hurl it out the cheery window.

Twenty minutes later, I was dressed and breakfasted and on my way to work. Strike accompanied me without threatening to shoot anyone, and I supposed I should count my blessings where I could.

I'd left the sentiment stones at home. Metcalf hadn't compelled me to keep them with me—not today anyway—and I figured I was less of a danger to everyone around me without Metcalf's magic at my literal fingertips.

But regardless of the sentiment stones' current whereabouts, things couldn't go on like this.

When I'd first decided to withhold information about my newly acquired chain magic, then the autopsy, the Lyrebird experiment, and what had happened with Dr. Yanders, I'd acted to protect myself.

Now I was more concerned about protecting others from *me*.

The magic stranglehold over my brain meant I couldn't tell anyone what Metcalf had done and revealed to me since then. Even thinking about relaying it to Gadson made my head ache with pressure. I felt trapped by the conflicting imperatives within me. Trapped by my desires that weren't mine at all.

I wanted nothing more than I wanted to obey Metcalf. But oh, I so badly wanted to warn my colleagues that I was compromised.

Of course, the parasite in my brain would win.

But the stuff that had happened before my cab ride with Metcalf, that stuff was uncovered by compulsion.

It wasn't a loophole or anything so useful as that. Metcalf's magic didn't allow for loopholes. The power sensed his full intentions and pressed it into his victim's mind without the need for clever wording—or any words at all. No, it was only that Metcalf was unconcerned about what I did with the information from the autopsy report and my visit with Dr. Yanders. Perhaps he assumed my colleagues already knew. Either way, he must believe it would make no difference to his plans.

Yet maybe my confession would make Gadson investigate the Lyrebird project and draw his own hypothesis about why Metcalf was after me. Or, at the very least, the captain's anger over my willful with-holding of evidence related to an active investigation might mean he'd keep an ill-tempered eye on me after that.

Maybe that would be enough.

Maybe it wouldn't.

Aurelis flew down to join me on the sidewalk when I was still a few minutes from the precinct.

"Any new gifts from Metcalf?" she asked.

I ducked my head, pretending to adjust my uniform to hide that fleeting blank look I'd observed on other mind-controlled puppets fighting against their compul-sions. Another point to the Metcalf parasite in my brain.

"Nope." And then, with the tug of awareness that I'd normally say more, "But with my favorite takeout place shut down, I ended up eating canned soup over the kitchen sink."

Aurelis snorted in amusement. "I had crispy Cantonese duck. Fifteen of them. Figured I deserved it after such a long day in my new supervisory role."

I didn't mention I'd only had the stomach for plain toast for breakfast.

"Hey, I think I'm going to talk to Gadson about the chain magic and the autopsy report and everything that came afterward. But—"

"*What?*"

It wasn't really a question.

"I should be able to keep you out of it. Imply you

didn't know, that I drove to San Bernardino and talked to the neurosurgeon on my own. I would've had just enough time after all."

"You think I'm worried about my own scales?" she snapped.

I hesitated. "Well, aren't you?"

"You're the one who'll have a target on your head if word gets out, Lyra. You think any company happy to abduct people and conduct lethal experiments on them is going to let you get on with your life if there's any chance of profit in it for them?"

I smiled grimly, thinking of my chain magic and the sentiment stone filled with Metcalf's power. "I'm not defenseless."

"The amount of times I've had to save your hide would say otherwise."

"Then maybe we'll get lucky and Metcalf and the FutureCorp assholes will trip over each other and take care of one of my problems for me."

Aurelis looked unconvinced. But she tossed her head and said with uncharacteristic coolness, "It's your life. I suppose you can trust whom you want with it."

An awkward silence followed. I was surprised she was so upset and wasn't entirely sure *why* she was reacting this way. I knew we were friends of a sort, but everything I'd read said dragons did not form deep relational bonds to other living beings. Only their hoards. Humans could be useful, and so interactions might occur on grounds of convenience, business, or entertainment. But it was transactional rather than relational. Oh, and I supposed they ate us sometimes, but that was a different sort of bond.

Maybe she was annoyed she'd gone to the trouble of flying me there and back to sate her curiosity and now I was giving away that hard-won intel for nothing.

We reached the station. "Thanks. For keeping my confidence."

But Aurelis didn't appear any less annoyed as I headed for Gadson's office.

The captain looked like he might have a coronary by the time I was done explaining. If it wouldn't have impeded the manhunt for Metcalf, I suspected Gadson would've dearly loved to suspend me again.

"I'll be checking into this, Ridley," he said after the vein at his temple had subsided a little. "Quietly. Now get your ass down to the intersection and take over for the poor sod who's been standing there for the past eight hours to keep up appearances."

"Yes, sir."

So no, unfortunately, my confession did not get me out of traffic duty.

Like the days before, the sun was unpleasantly hot, the fumes unpleasantly noxious, and the drivers unpleasantly irritable. I rotated the sign, waved my arms, and sweated a lot. I'd have to do laundry soon.

The work was just as mind-numbingly boring as I remembered. But today I at least appreciated the temporary cease-fire on the war within me. Metcalf's only compulsion within this context was to carry on my duties as normal, which aligned with my own well enough.

Yes, there was still a risk he'd turn me against my colleagues, but if he was arrogant enough to come here and give me his next dirty assignment, we might have a chance at taking him down.

Provided someone within the tactical team could recognize him, that is. Had they anticipated he might be using glamour or heavy disguise?

Aurelis might be able to see through fae glamour. I'd never actually asked her. But her nose was stuck in one of the books she'd brought, and I knew how single-minded she could be. Especially since she was still vexed with me.

Strike likewise hadn't forgiven me for not bringing her into the MMA stadium last night. I'd explained private drones weren't allowed inside, but she'd spent the time in the waiting area streaming live feeds and learning more about the sport than I ever cared to know.

Turns out my personal protection drone had an appetite for blood. All this time I'd thought she'd been programmed to be overly suspicious, but now I wondered if she'd just been looking for an excuse to blow stuff up.

And she accused *me* of being irrational.

I was sucking down another mouthful of lukewarm water when a yellow panel van broke from the crawling lines of traffic to stop haphazardly on the curb. Bold stencil-style flowers covered the rear and sides of the van's paintwork, and a man with shoulder-length auburn hair glossier and better groomed than mine climbed out.

"Sir, you can't park there," I yelled over the street noise and thrum of old engines.

"Not parking," he yelled back with an easy smile. "Just dropping off a delivery for you. Officer Ridley, right?"

He stepped to the side of the van without pausing for confirmation and slid open the door.

I tensed, waiting to see what he'd pull out of there. After everything that had happened lately, I was feeling twitchy. But when the man reemerged, it was with a huge arrangement of red roses like in some corny Valentine's Day movie.

He lugged the arrangement toward me, the same easy smile on his face. "Officer Lyra Ridley, I'm assuming? My delivery instructions were quite specific..."

I glanced behind me to ensure the flow of traffic was continuing without my helpful arm gestures. "Right. But—"

A connection fired in my brain. The memory of Miles listing out all the questions Ronan's parents had asked about me—questions that had included my favorite flowers.

Surely not...

And no way would Miles have told them red roses anyway.

That was when a bolt of something like lightning struck the deliveryman in a blaze of arcing white light.

He spasmed in place as if being zapped with a high-powered Taser, and behind me cars skidded to a stop while others tried to speed up, resulting in a cacophony of honking and shouted insults about their fellow drivers' parentage.

The "lightning" was coming from my personal protection drone. The flowers and the deliveryman's jacket were beginning to smoke.

"Strike! What are you doing? Stop it!"

"I am following your orders, Lyra," she said calmly. "He is aiming a weapon at you."

My eyes flew over the spasming stranger again, but both of his hands were holding the now ruined flower arrangement.

"Roses are not a weapon. Stop it. Now. That's an order."

"Not until you train your firearm on him. Don't worry, my innovative lightning immobilizer is not lethal. In theory."

In theory? But going along with my crazy drone's demands was probably the fastest way to end this. I yanked out my gun and trained it on the poor guy who must now be having a worse day than I was.

The lightning magitech thing shut off, and Strike dove down and smashed the flower arrangement onto the asphalt.

The abused petals and leaves disintegrated on

impact, and nestled in the middle of the now barren stems was a compact handgun.

"Hands on your head. Now!" I snapped.

The delivery guy raised trembling arms and placed them—after one or two tries—on his heavily disheveled hair.

"Don't shoot," he rasped. "The devil made me do it."

I almost laughed.

Metcalf. Seriously?

But my bemusement quickly turned to understanding. And when it did, I wished for that blissful ignorance back.

I'd been wrong yesterday. Metcalf wasn't just playing on another game board altogether. He was playing *both* games. Or at least he was putting a token effort toward the old game to keep those tasked with hunting him focused in the wrong direction.

What better way to keep law enforcement exactly where he wanted them so he could pursue his real goal unhindered?

A goal that included laying waste to Washington, and who knew what else.

The plainclothes positioned in plain sight around my location were clearly still playing. They'd waited it out, not wanting to blow their covers for a single delivery guy. Which meant it was still just me, Strike, and Aurelis out here.

So I played along too. I cuffed the dazed florist and

passed him off to a reluctant Aurelis to guard until the precinct sent someone to pick him up.

Then I returned to traffic duty.

I was grateful Strike had saved me. Really I was. But I couldn't help thinking just a little wistfully about how hospitals had air-conditioning.

CHAPTER EIGHTEEN

Someone knocked on the door. I'd gotten home from work, taken another shower, and was halfway through examining the piteous contents of my fridge and freezer when I heard it. The sound made me start like a wet cat and drop the packet of freezer-burned kale that'd been there since the day I'd moved in.

Yet for a welcome change, I wasn't compelled to let in whoever was knocking. So I chucked the kale back in the freezer, then walked over to peer out the peephole.

Was that *Ronan*? And was he carrying *cookies*?

My hand was on the latch before my next thought brought it to an abrupt halt.

The delivery guy today had come bearing gifts too.

Worse, Metcalf could look like anyone he wanted.

I stood there in frozen indecision so long that Ronan, if it was really him, knocked a second time.

Metcalf wouldn't have the patience to have waited,

surely? But no, Metcalf had endless patience when it suited his purposes.

"Lyra?" Ronan called uncertainly. "Are you all right? I know you're on the other side of the door."

I loosed a breath. It was Ronan's voice. Fae glamour didn't extend to voices.

Even so, I should be on guard. I couldn't imagine how Metcalf could've gotten to Ronan in Faerie. But Metcalf had already done the impossible and managed to wrestle one fae under his control.

Or—for all I knew, maybe the bastard had found some hapless being with voice-altering magic.

"Prove it's really you," I called, jamming my eye against the peephole again.

"Um. Okay." He repositioned the heaped plate of cookies as if he found their meager weight cumbersome. "The first time we met, you shot a troll in the foot, saved me from drowning, then got very bossy afterward and forced the poor wounded troll to carry me over his shoulder like a sack of soggy potatoes. It was all most annoying."

I grinned and swung the door open. Some of that intel would've been obtainable by Metcalf, but the annoyance was all Ronan.

"Soggy *poisoned* potatoes," I corrected. "And it almost sounds like you don't *still* find me annoying."

His lips twitched. "Well, I'm adult enough to admit you grew on me. Your family is still in the annoying phase."

I shrugged unsympathetically. "If you gave Archer cotton candy, you've got only yourself to blame."

I beckoned him inside, checked to make sure Strike was keeping an eye on him while I turned my back, and locked the door.

"Who is this?" Strike asked me.

"A friend."

"He's much more conventionally attractive than your usual visitor."

Ronan raised an eyebrow. "Usual visitor?"

"Never mind," I snapped before Strike could say anything she shouldn't. "Ronan, this is Strike, my experimental personal protection drone."

"I find Lyra annoying sometimes too," she said.

I gaped at her. "Excuse me? Do you even have emotions?"

"I can extrapolate from the available data."

Ronan's lips twitched again.

I shook my head and made the mistake of looking around my apartment. It was a lot messier than usual. Somehow I'd had more important things on my mind lately than cleaning. And the mess extended to me too. I wasn't sweaty anymore, but my hair was wet and tangled, and I'd pulled on my most comfy and therefore most tatty lounging-about-the-house clothes.

At least I hadn't left the sentiment stones out in plain sight. I'd buried them in a drawer, not wanting to look at them.

Except that was the parasite thinking. It would have

been *good* if Ronan had seen them and been given cause for suspicion. Ugh.

"Um, not that I'm not glad to see you, but to what do I owe this surprise visit?"

I realized then that he was still holding his armful of baked goods and that I hadn't invited him to sit or offered him anything to drink.

"I mean, make yourself comfortable. Please. Can I get you a drink? And um, would you like to set that down or—"

"These are for you," Ronan announced almost as awkwardly as me and thrust the plate of cookies in my direction.

"Oh thanks."

Upon closer inspection, the cookies were rich, golden, buttery perfection scattered with chunks of something darker, and they smelled even better than Ronan did, which was saying something. "Did your household cook make these?"

"No. I baked them myself."

I gawked at him. Call me crazy, but I'd never imagined the grave and powerful Lord Ronan Nightwing puttering around a kitchen in an apron, baking sweets. It would have to be a larger kitchen than mine to avoid swiping things off the countertops with his wings, I reflected. Still, the picture was wholesome and cozy and melted some of the tension I'd been carrying everywhere with me for the past three days.

Ronan seemed unsure what to do with his hands now that he'd passed over the goodies.

What on earth was he *doing* here?

Surely Metcalf wouldn't put him up to this. Not unless the cookies contained some unknown Faerie substance that increased neuroplasticity or something.

But the unfortunate reality was that Metcalf didn't *need* help turning me into his loyal sidekick.

"I usually do my own cooking," Ronan explained to my too-long silence. "But after you warned not to let your father in the kitchen, I thought it would be wise to hire a professional for the time being." He shrugged. "Anyway, it's hard to go wrong with toffee made from windflower nectar."

I shoved away the image of Ronan in the kitchen and hustled to my own. "Well, thanks. They look and smell amazing. What did you say you'd like to drink?"

"Coffee please."

I poured us both one and selected a few of the cookies to go with them since I knew all too well I had nothing better to offer. Not unless Ronan had an unusual predilection for freezer-burned kale anyway. Then I returned to the living room to find Ronan still standing. Hadn't I told him to make himself comfortable?

Oh, his *wings*. What did winged fae like to sit on? Mossy logs in dappled glades? Noble mythical steeds ready to charge into battle? I recalled him looking uncomfortable perched on the edge of a plastic chair in my hospital room.

"Oh, um, would you like a barstool to sit on?"

"The couch is fine." He removed his sword and sat down as if to prove it to me, settling his wings neatly against the cushioned backrest and looking surprisingly comfortable.

Wait. *Sword?* How had I failed to notice he was wearing a sword? Had it been glamoured? Or had I really been so focused on the cookies (and, okay, *him*) that I'd just not noticed?

I forced myself not to stare at it. If he'd wanted—or had been compelled—to chop my head off, he'd had plenty of opportunity already. Instead, I handed him his drink.

"You're the one doing *me* the favor," I reminded him as I handed him his drink. "Why are you bringing me cookies?"

"For an excuse to get out of the house?"

I narrowed my eyes. "Not buying it. I mean, not that you might want to avoid going home at the moment, but that you couldn't come up with a better excuse to do it."

He shrugged eloquently.

I tasted the cookies.

My eyes rolled into the back of my head with near orgasmic pleasure as crispy caramelized edges set off the soft, buttery, melt-in-your-mouth centers and the most delectable toffee I'd ever tasted dissolved against my tongue. I polished it off faster than was polite and eyed the rest of the plate I'd brought over.

I may have been salivating.

"These are *incredible.* Seriously, if your feathers didn't make me sneeze, I'd ask you to marry me for a lifetime of cookies like that."

Ronan dropped his mug. It shattered on impact, flinging coffee and ceramic shards all over the floor.

Hot liquid dripped down Ronan's legs, the side of the couch, the coffee table, and basically everything in a two-yard radius. "Sorry. I'll clean that up." He drew on his endlessly versatile fae magic. The coffee extracted itself obediently from fabric and floor while the ceramic shards drew back together into a neat pile and reassembled themselves. Liquid conglomerated into a single giant droplet hovering a few inches above the ground and he scooped it back into the restored mug.

I managed not to stare. At his magic or the uneaten cookie resting on his knee.

"Um, let me get you another drink."

He sprang to his feet. "No need. I really just came to drop those cookies off."

I narrowed my eyes as he disappeared into the kitchen. I didn't believe that for a minute.

"By the way, do you have any updates on how long you'll need to take Metcalf down?"

Aha! *That's* what he was doing here. Not so subtly trying to figure out how much longer he'd have to be inconvenienced for.

Mystery solved. I probably deserved another cookie for that.

Unfortunately, I didn't have the news he was hoping to hear. "A whole team of us is on it full time, but there's no way to predict what will happen or when."

He returned from the kitchen, his face so neutral I suspected he was working at keeping it that way. "All right. Well, I'd better go. But feel free to come visit your family sometime."

"Sure. Or even better, take them back, right?"

I caught a flash of a smile before he left and chalked it up as a win. Then I returned to my freezer to dig out my last ready-made meal.

Which was when I noticed my ice cream was missing.

Could Ronan really have just stolen my *ice cream*?

Surely not. And yet I swear it had been in the freezer a minute ago. Plus if Strike had taken it upon herself to "protect" me from myself, I should've been able to find it in the trash.

It wasn't in the trash.

Wondering whether I'd absentmindedly picked it up and carried it with me to answer the door, I retraced my steps, checking any surface I might've plonked it down on.

That was when I spotted Ronan's sword lying across the couch.

I dialed his number.

"You left your sword here."

"Ah. That's all right. I'll pick it up another time."

Another time? Was he thinking of visiting regularly now?

Part of me was foolishly pleased with the idea, but most of me was terrified he'd run into Metcalf and be unable to protect himself outside the bounds of Faerie.

Of course, I couldn't warn him.

"Fine, another time then. I'll try not to cut myself on it in the interim." I paused. "Um, this is going to sound strange, but... you didn't happen to take my ice cream, did you?"

Dead silence answered me.

"Ronan? Are you there?"

"Sorry. I thought you just accused me of stealing your ice cream?"

I flushed. "Never mind. Thanks again for the cookies!"

I disconnected as fast as I could and returned to being totally baffled by his visit and my still-very-missing ice cream.

CHAPTER NINETEEN

Two days passed with no further visits from Metcalf.

Traffic duty was stupidly boring. But Stewie was at last released on bail, no other florists tried to shoot me, and I at least managed to catch up on sleep. Some of it while standing in the middle of the intersection…

Did I mention work was boring?

But I knew better than to get comfortable. I spent every hour in a weird limbo of nauseating dread and dreary monotony. Any moment Metcalf could crash back into my life and shatter any or everything I held dear.

Then he did.

He came for me at night. But this time we didn't stay in my apartment.

I was sitting on my couch, trying to tune into the TV instead of the fears in my head, when I felt the sudden need to collect my blood-won sentiment stones, go downstairs, and hop in the waiting cab.

We traveled in silence, Metcalf, the fae woman, and me. The cabbie didn't talk either. And by the time I got out of the vehicle onto a busy stretch of the Strip, we were all wearing other people's faces.

The glimpse of my unfamiliar reflection in the glass made my stride falter. But Strike's reflection hovered beside mine, unchanged, and I found a peculiar comfort in that.

We entered one of the ritzy hotels in the heart of the Strip, and the fae woman waved a card over the security panel and pressed the button for the top floor.

The penthouse.

How was it possible that someone on the run—a wanted criminal every cop and most civilians were looking out for—was living it up in a penthouse suite?

Anger burned in my veins as I stood meekly beside Metcalf in the elevator. But of course, he didn't *look* like Metcalf.

The fae so rarely left Faerie that there were no commonly used safeguards against their glamour. Why would there be? The real question was how had Metcalf managed to sink his mental claws into one? And why weren't Faerie arbiters searching for her?

As if guessing my thoughts, Metcalf smiled. "Did you expect me to be slumming it? Mind you, it's a touch tiresome having to relocate every day. But I'll leave this dust bowl of a city soon enough, and by then the world will have bigger problems to occupy itself with than hunting me."

His leaving my city sounded good at first glance, but that last part scared me witless.

The elevator's doors opened directly into the penthouse. The huge, sweeping space with its own outdoor rooftop entertaining area and 180-degree views of the city skyline was designed to impress. But I barely noticed the warm timber floors and luxurious rugs, the expensive furnishings, or the meticulously selected art.

Because there were twenty people there waiting for us.

I amended my previous question. How was it possible an infamous criminal like Metcalf was living it up in a penthouse suite... with twenty missing members of the public?

There was no apparent pattern or uniformity to those Metcalf had chosen, although most of them were human. Presumably because we were easier to acquire and control. The only thing that matched were their expressions of weary apprehension as they waited to see what their unwanted dictator would force them to do next.

Metcalf gestured at the nearest cluster of them—a young man about my age wearing an ill-fitting suit, a feminine-presenting individual decked out in a sparkling green dress somewhere north of forty, and a woman in pastel joggers who likely qualified for senior discounts.

"That one can make himself and anyone he's touching completely invisible from technological surveillance. The one in the dress has fire magic that could make your dragon blush. And the old lady has some weird magical bond to her gun that makes sure she *never* misses."

He pointed at the next figure. This one familiar because it was his likeness that Metcalf had been wearing on the way here. "That guy's magic is useless, but he's a tourist with very deep pockets, so he's footing the bill for the penthouse without drawing attention."

Metcalf's introductions were telling. These people he'd ripped from their lives and forced into obedience were not *people* to him. He saw them as tools. Tools he could pick up and wield for his purposes—then discard when their usefulness ran out with no more thought than someone else would give to throwing out a paper towel. Another classic characteristic of a psychopath.

I tried to memorize each face and any detail Metcalf let slip, hoping I might be able to free these people from the self-proclaimed devil's clutches. And knowing if I ever had a chance to take Metcalf down, these individuals might be my unwilling adversaries.

The devil shifted to introduce the next of his tools and then shrugged. "Eh. It doesn't matter what they are. Most of them will be dead in a few days anyway."

My throat was thick with suppressed anger. Anger... and fear. But I didn't say anything—even though my tongue was under my control. What was the point?

Or was that just an excuse for my cowardice?

Metcalf fixed his unfeeling gaze on me. "But I'll be taking *you* with me. And the fae too even though she's more challenging to manage than the average weak-minded human."

She didn't react to this proclamation. Had she already known? Or was she so tightly leashed she couldn't even change her expression?

"For now, we're going to make sure you can wield my magic well enough to handle a group rather than just an individual."

His eyes roamed over the penthouse and his gathered prisoners like a bratty toddler surveying the toys he was about to break.

"You will force everyone to fight. Leaving you and the fae out of it. MMA rules apply, eh? No weapons. No magic. Just the age-old tradition of flesh against flesh."

His calculating gaze returned to me. "Making them hurt each other isn't the real challenge. Deep down, every human has the desire for violence. We just bring it to the surface."

I vehemently disagreed.

Silently.

"The real test will be overriding their reflexive need to scream when they're hurt." He flashed his teeth at me. "Do both, Lyra. We wouldn't want to wake the neighbors…"

Then his magic lashed me. And I wanted what he wanted. Wanted to see if I could do it.

186

My hand reached for the sentiment stone he'd had me fill. The non-parasite part of my brain wanted me to smash his skull with it. But as always, *his* will won out.

The stone provided with perfect recall the sensation of Metcalf's magic under my fingers, and I shifted my attention to the twenty people still waiting under the dictator's thrall. Their expressions of weary apprehension had shifted to fear.

Metcalf had made sure they'd heard what was coming. Said it aloud to draw out their suffering along with mine.

Except my own fear was diminished now, beaten down by the overwhelming need to test myself.

So I did.

One side of the room turned on the other in a crash of bodies more disturbing for its quiet. Like some unsettling pantomime where the fury and distress on their faces and the frantic, frenzied blows were convincing yet incomplete. It was so jarring as to feel surreal, accompanied as it was by no more sound than the thud of flesh meeting flesh and the ragged breathing of the participants.

But the damage was all too real.

Without doing more than twitching a finger, I'd just coerced a roomful of people—people whose names I did not know and backgrounds I did not understand—into savage brutality.

The majority fought with more desperation than skill, clawing at hair, at eyes, at clothes, punching with inexperienced fists. It was enough to make them bruise and bleed and maybe break some of the more fragile bones like ribs and noses. But relatively unlikely to kill. Although I was excruciatingly aware all it took was a little mischance and even an inexperienced fighter could accidentally end a life.

No one screamed.

But there were three among the twenty who *did* have combat experience. I could tell by the brute efficiency with which they brought the others down. A leg sweep that probably resulted in a concussion. A blow to the face that broke someone's nose. A punch to another's throat that had them clawing for breath.

None of those victims screamed either.

One scrappy guy—the young man in the ill-fitting suit Metcalf had introduced first—put up more of a fight than the others. One of the experienced combatants took him down in a calculated kick that bent his knee in a direction it was never supposed to go. The snap of bone cracked through the air of the stately penthouse.

But even he did not scream.

Metcalf applauded slowly, and I let the room-wide brawl stop as abruptly as it had begun. The fighters stood in place or lay where they'd fallen, panting and bleeding quietly as overwhelming compulsion was replaced with shock and unfiltered pain.

My hand recoiled from the stone, and the guy with the ruined knee started screaming. A sound that was cut off almost instantly by Metcalf. The man curled up in agony, tears streaming down his bloodless cheeks, but only whimpers emerged from his throat after that.

The experienced combatant who'd inflicted the injury on him sat down suddenly. Dismay at what she'd done written clear across her face.

Metcalf, however, was smiling again.

"Very good, little lyrebird. Very good. Looks like the broken one there is our lucky winner. Well, unlucky for him I suppose. But I've been meaning to test out your *other* method of magic acquisition. It's time to learn whether your little trick with the chain mage was a one-off glitch or something we can replicate to our advantage."

Whatever he saw on my face made him smile wider.

"Ah. You didn't realize I knew that part, huh? Your homeless friend was most forthcoming. And part of the reason I toyed with you on day one was to see it for myself, given I didn't judge him to be the most reliable source. It wasn't *all* fun and games."

The smile slipped from his face, replaced by callous intent.

"Put him out of his misery. And use both his and my magic while you do it."

A fresh compulsion invaded my brain, and horror almost brought me to my knees as my worst fears were realized.

He wanted me to kill the injured man.

A man who could easily be healed at the nearest hospital.

To learn whether I could steal his magic permanently as I'd done with the chain mage.

My hand shifted for my gun.

"Use this," the devil said. And handed me a garrote.

CHAPTER TWENTY

No, the uncontaminated part of my mind screamed. *Don't do this. You can't do this.*

But my traitorous hand took the crude garrote from Metcalf, and my stupid legs carried me toward the young man weeping and writhing in agony on the expensive silk rug.

He wants me to use the garrote so I don't get blood on the carpet, a distant, detached part of me noted.

Neither side of my brain cared about that detail.

Kill him. Take his power. Take Metcalf's power too, if you can.

My vision blurred with tears I hadn't noticed I was crying. But I was still walking toward the prone figure, the nylon cord dangling from my fingers.

Strangling was not a nice way to go. I knew from personal experience. Some nights I still woke up from fragmented regurgitations of that chain squeezing my airway closed. It was slow, for a start. The garrote would make it quicker, but it would still take ten to fifteen seconds for the victim to lose consciousness. And those seconds would be filled with the instinctive violent terror of being denied air.

You can't do this, my own mind pleaded again. *You can't kill someone in cold blood.*

But I was going to.

I tried to fight the compulsion. To comb through the hundreds of reasons not to kill him. To divert the murderous compulsion in Metcalf's direction instead of the poor man he'd painted a target on.

I even thought about turning it on myself. If I grabbed my gun now—before I got to the anti-surveillance mage—could I incapacitate myself so completely the compulsion wouldn't be possible?

Strike was here somewhere. Maybe if I turned the gun on myself, *she* could incapacitate me.

But my hand stubbornly resisted my urging.

I was sobbing now. Only a yard from the man I was about to kill. Snot bubbled from one of my nostrils, and my eyes stung from tears.

The guy in the ill-fitting suit tried to drag himself away from me. But all movement inflicted further agony on his ruined knee.

Would Strike stop me?

No. She was *my* personal protection drone. Which meant she wouldn't intervene unless it was my life in jeopardy.

Don't.

I reached for the sentiment stone again. *Be still,* I willed the man. *Don't panic. I'll try to make it quick.*

I doubted that last part would translate through Metcalf's magic. But I found I could whisper it. "I'm sorry," I breathed as I stepped around his broken leg and slipped the garrote around his neck. "I'll try to make it quick."

Through the brush of my fingers against his throat, I felt my magic reshaping to match his. As Metcalf ordered, I used it, even though there probably weren't any cameras watching except for Strike.

Then I released the sentiment stone, took up both ends of the garrote, and drew it tight.

He didn't struggle.

I used Metcalf's ebbing magic to make sure of it.

And when it was done, we both collapsed onto that expensive rug.

I don't know how long I stayed there. The man's head resting on my knees. If Strike or the other captives reacted, I didn't hear it.

I didn't hear anything except the pounding of blood in my ears. Didn't see anything except the man's sightless, bulging brown eyes staring up at me in accusation.

Someone dumped cold water over my head.

I didn't react.

Didn't move until Metcalf's magic compelled me to.

"Well?" he demanded. "Did it work? Do you have either of our magics now?"

I blinked stupidly until he compelled me to try it. First to draw on his own mind-control magic without touching the sentiment stone.

Nothing happened.

And even through the shock, I felt a distant dribble of relief. That I hadn't been saddled with his evil magic forever. That I hadn't taken yet another step closer to becoming the fanatically loyal and all-too-useful sidekick he wanted.

Then he held up a smartphone and sent another compulsion into me.

I tried to draw on the dead man's magic this time.

No. Not dead. *Murdered.*

By me.

And when I reached for that foreign new power I'd just been introduced to, I found it waiting for me.

Metcalf tapped the screen a few times and flipped the phone around. It was in video mode, with the phone's front camera facing toward me.

I could only tell it was the front camera being used because the screen showed the windows behind me, rather than the elevator doors behind Metcalf.

I, according to the phone, did not exist.

Metcalf pocketed the device, looking smug.

"Fascinating."

He looked over the rest of his "tools" with a clinical eye.

"It's a shame we don't know how many magic abilities you can acquire before your brain hemorrhages like the other lyrebirds. Or even whether that's a risk for you. Otherwise I could consolidate my assets and have you kill everyone else right now."

He shook his head. "But there'll be time for experimentation later. After you and I have orchestrated a long-overdue world war."

I was too shell-shocked for his words to sink in. My brain snared in an unending loop of horror.

Irked by my lack of reaction to his dramatic pronouncement, Metcalf sent me home in disgust.

CHAPTER TWENTY-ONE

Two days passed.

I tried to tell myself it was not my fault. That I was a victim too.

But *I* was still alive.

I still had hope of rescue.

That man whose name I did not know would never hope for anything again.

Metcalf's compulsions wouldn't allow me to call in sick. But I had three rostered days off, and I spent them lying in bed, lying on the couch, and when that felt too forgiving, lying on the floor.

Which was what I was doing when Ronan visited for the second time...

CHAPTER TWENTY-TWO

I glanced down at myself to make sure I was at least wearing pants and rubbed at the imprint of the floor on my cheek. Then remembered that Ronan had known I was standing awkwardly on the other side of the door last time, and opened it.

"Ronan," I greeted him, surprised at the small spark of warmth I felt at seeing him standing in my hallway.

It was the first thing I'd felt in days that wasn't horror, shame, and fear.

Metcalf's compulsion or my own volition—I wasn't sure which—made me grapple for something normal to say. "Did my family run you out of your house again?"

"Actually"—he looked at the floor, perhaps trying to match it to the indentations on my cheek—"I came to ask a favor."

My brows shot up. "Oh?"

He cleared his throat. "Would you accompany me to a... work event? Um, in Faerie?"

"I can't," I blurted, fear coating my insides with ice. I couldn't go anywhere *near* my family so long as Metcalf controlled my actions. But I couldn't tell Ronan that. "I'm busy that night. Sorry."

"I haven't told you when it is," Ronan stated flatly.

Was that a flicker of hurt I saw before his features turned neutral?

It didn't matter. Because I couldn't change my answer.

Ronan sighed. "Can I come in? You need to know all the facts before making a decision."

I cringed at my rudeness and stepped aside so he could enter. "Yes. Of course. Sorry."

He trailed me into the open living area.

"Can I get you something? A, um..." I didn't have anything to offer. The cookies were long gone, and I'd been subsisting on canned goods. Strike had been extremely judgy about it. "A drink?" I finished.

"No. I'm fine. Sorry for, uh, waking you?"

It wasn't quite a question, so I pretended not to hear it. No need to correct the assumption that my state of disarray was because I'd been sleeping in the middle of the day.

I flopped into one of my armchairs, and Ronan perched on my couch.

"Remember when you asked whether I'd had to

promise the border authorities my firstborn to get your family into Faerie at the drop of a hat?"

That didn't sound good.

"Yeah?"

"Right. So... I didn't have to sell the soul of my unborn child. But I did have to, well, pretend I was courting you."

I'd begun to slump back into the cushions, but that made me jolt upright. "What?"

"Over the course of modern history, Faerie governance has shifted from four warmongering fae monarchies to consolidating those monarchies into one and, more recently, into a sort of democratic council system, which stands alongside the king or queen and gives representation to all fae-kin. The upheavals have left us with a strange mix of the contemporary system and a smattering of mostly obsolete archaic laws that no one's gotten around to changing. Anyway, under the current rule, vampires are not allowed in Faerie. It doesn't say so anywhere in the legislation, but if a vampire applies for a visa, they're always denied. And even without the complication of your father's species, instantaneous visas don't just happen."

I listened with increasing discomfort. I'd had no idea how much I was asking when I'd called in Ronan's favor.

But even if I had, I'd still have asked.

Because I needed to protect my family at any cost. And if I hadn't, they would have been here. Easy pickings for Metcalf.

I sat on my hands to stop them from betraying my discomfort. "I see."

Ronan nodded. "So I used one of the archaic laws to get around those restrictions. Because of all the aforementioned warmongering, there was this custom where if two fae from different sides of the conflict were courting, either one of the couple could offer their intended and their intended's immediate family sanctuary in their own estate. And no one would interfere."

"Ah."

A lot of peculiar things suddenly made sense. Why Ronan had invited my family to stay at his own home instead of a hotel. Why he'd seemed so uncomfortable when I'd casually mentioned that I hoped it hadn't been too much trouble. And maybe why—

"Does this have something to do with the cookies you brought?"

I could've sworn he blushed.

"Yes. To, uh, maintain the appearance of our courtship, there are certain customs I had to observe. One of them is the exchange of food and a treasured weapon from each party. It represents a promise to sustain and protect one another."

"Wait. *Exchange?* So it *was* you who stole my ice cream!"

"*Exchanged*," he reiterated firmly, objecting to my implication of theft. "And there was hardly anything left in the tub. I also borrowed your personal handgun."

My jaw dropped. I hadn't even noticed since I'd been using my work-issued weapons as usual.

"…And also why I accidentally on purpose left my sword here," Ronan finished.

Now *I* might have been the one blushing. I mean, I'd known something was up, but all my theories had been way off base.

Plus I'd sort of been hoping it might be, at least in part, because Ronan liked my company. Rather than that he'd been obligated to bring me cookies in some antiquated charade of *pretending* to like my company just to honor a debt.

Ronan cleared his throat again.

"Anyway. I'd been hoping your team might have captured Metcalf before now, and I wouldn't have to admit any of this to you. But unless you have good news for me…?"

I suppressed a shudder. Barely. And shook my head, not trusting myself to speak.

"Then I'm afraid you must accompany me to this event. If you don't, people are going to start asking questions, and those questions are going to get your family kicked out of Faerie."

I didn't suppress the shudder this time. "No. They can't. They have to stay safe."

It was the only thing keeping me from completely falling apart.

"When is it?"

"Tonight."

I scowled at him.

"What if I had plans?" Extremely unlikely right now, but still. "What if I was working?"

"Your father told me you were rostered off."

My scowl lessened as I realized Ronan springing it on me last minute might be my saving grace. It meant Metcalf had only a small window in which to discover what was happening and compel me to do something awful.

I expelled a breath. "Fine. You said it was a work event?"

Ronan winced. "Well, sort of. More like a formal gathering of the privileged and powerful in Faerie with pretentious music, a pretentious dress code, and pretentious dancing."

I stared at him. "You mean like a *ball?*"

"Yes."

A new, novel form of distress was unfurling in my gut. I owned exactly one pair of heels, impractical torture contraptions that they were. And my all-purpose formal ink-blue dress for weddings, functions, and funerals had suffered a fatal accident the last time I'd donned it.

"Did you say dress code?"

"Yes."

"What on earth do Faerie citizens wear to—"

"I took the liberty of bringing you something."

"Oh." I wasn't sure how I felt about that. Relieved mostly, but irritated too.

Strike, who'd remained blissfully quiet and unobtrusive until that moment, flew forward until she almost bumped into Ronan's chest. "Can I come too? My programming makes me curious about new experiences, and there isn't any second or even thirdhand data available about this one."

Ronan blinked a few times, obviously flummoxed.

"I don't mind dressing up," she added cheerfully.

CHAPTER TWENTY-THREE

Ronan's "work event" was held in a starlit clearing fringed with stately silver trees. The night was mild with a warm, sweet-smelling breeze, and the verdant grass and delicate blue wildflowers underfoot remained untrampled no matter how many feet passed over them.

There was no need for artificial lighting. The stars overhead shone brighter than I'd ever seen, as if the heavens themselves were celebrating. And thousands of the Faerie equivalent of fireflies, tiny glowing figures somewhere between humanoid and insect, eddied gently among the guests, illuminating the clearing in pale golden light.

Ronan hadn't been kidding about the dress code.

Most of the male fae I saw were clad in ornate formal armor, the formfitting interlocking plates accentuating the shape of their powerful torsos and lending the wearers an aura of solemn dignity. Elaborate engravings, often inlaid with striking color, held the weight and meaning of generations rather than acting as mere decoration. The overall effect was *decidedly* flattering.

But the fae women were far from overshadowed. Elegant ball gowns embellished with glamour or magic shifted and swayed mesmerizingly even while the wearers were standing still. Some sported exaggerated full skirts or oversized trains that only a bride might dream of wearing without magic to ensure the layers would never get tangled or trod on. One woman wore a scarlet gown with a skirt of living roses growing up to meet her waist. Another fashion-forward individual was covered by a thin layer of frost, somehow woven in the ghostly outline of a gown, and a thick layer of ice-colored jewelry.

A number of fae bucked the gendered conventions, some men wearing flowing fashion statements with devastating effect, and many women opting for formal armor instead of ball gowns. Regardless of their attire, only about one in five of the fae were winged.

And then there were the fae-kin. A dryad whose branches were blooming with soft pink petals. A gremlin weighed down with so many elaborate jeweled weapons I was surprised they weren't sinking into the soil with every step. A river troll wearing what I presumed was his very best water weed loincloth and some coating on his teeth that shimmered gold. A sprite adorned only in the tumbling locks of her own blue hair that she'd threaded with fine lace-like copper chains. A kelpie whose dripping black coat smelled fresh and wild like an incoming storm rather than stagnant water and mildew, her hooves polished mirror bright.

It was beautiful and wondrous and surreal. And more than a little intimidating.

Ronan's armor was an understated matte black, matched to his splendid wings, the elegant black-on-black engravings subtly embellished with thread-thin gold trim.

My dress was relatively understated too. And I was grateful Ronan hadn't drawn any more attention to me than necessary. The gown was a soft pale gray with a fitted bodice and a flowing A-line skirt that had enough layers that I fit in, but not so many that I felt like I was traipsing about with a giant traffic cone around my legs. Those layers shifted in an ever-changing array of muted colors as I walked, like spider silk catching the sunlight. The gown was long enough to hide my heels but sadly too long for me to sneakily wear flats.

Strike was—thank goodness for small mercies—*not* wearing a dress.

But despite our decidedly *un*-attention-grabbing clothing, heads turned at our approach. Then the whispers started, spreading through the crowd like quicksilver, which led to more assessing gazes and murmured words I couldn't catch. In tongues I could not understand unless the speaker wished me to.

I felt my spine stiffen under the weight of those gazes, but I kept my expression neutral. "They're acting like you've never brought a date before."

"I haven't," Ronan said shortly. "I've never brought a drone either."

I raised an eyebrow. "And why is that?"

He grimaced. "Solitude suits me, and it also makes my job simpler."

"Oh? What do you do exactly when you're not holidaying with a bunch of murderous cult members in Nevada?"

"I'm an emissary for the Governing Council."

I made an exaggerated go-on gesture.

He looked pained. "Which means I go wherever they send me to do whatever they need me to do. Usually *within* Faerie's borders. Investigation. Dispute resolution. Enforcement. Whatever. All of it requires me to be impartial. Which is a great deal easier without relational entanglements."

"Sounds kind of lonely."

"There's nothing wrong with doing life alone."

"Of course not. So long as that's what makes you happy."

"I'm happy," he grumbled in a tone that was assuredly not.

I hid a smile. "You're positively glowing with it."

He growled low in his throat. "I'm certainly no happier with your family underfoot. And because of you, my parents keep inviting themselves over. Which is worse."

I didn't hide my amusement this time. "They can be a lot to handle," I admitted. "But I'd prefer to have my hands *and* heart full than go through life without them. Are your parents really that bad?"

"However bad you're thinking, multiply it by a factor of ten. And they'll want to meet you, so consider yourself warned."

Nerves fluttered in my stomach—like I was about to meet the parents of a man I was *actually* dating.

"All right. New topic then. What *does* make you happy?"

He stared at me as if I'd sprouted a second head. Could that happen in Faerie? I touched my neck surreptitiously to check.

"You're a *people person*," he accused. "That's probably why you're so chirpy all the time too."

I had a flashback of lying on the floor. "Just answer my question."

"Not being forced to attend pretentious events like this one."

I bit back a grin. To my relief, none of the glamorous gossipers had approached us, and somehow the crankier Ronan got, the more cheerful I felt. This was the most fun I'd had in weeks. And the majority of me was all too glad to throw myself into it and forget about... everything else for a while.

"Well, you're here now," I pointed out helpfully. "You might as well make the best of it."

"I'd prefer to be fed on by a flotilla of piranha pixies."

I fought back another smirk. "That's always a fall-back option. But maybe you should try it my way first."

"How?" he bit out.

"That depends on whatever floats your boat. Stuff your face on the food that I presume is amazing. Or hide in the bushes and throw a selection of entrées at your parents. Find a pretty woman—or anyone on the gender spectrum that suits your preferences—and flirt your heart out. Invent amusing conversations between other guests for your own entertainment. Or bribe one of the firefly thingies to keep landing on your father's nose all night."

His lips were twitching. So I kept going.

"Look, I'll go first. See that couple over there? The woman in the ivy dress and emerald-crusted tiara having a heated one-way conversation with her partner?"

Her partner was almost hunched by fae standards, listening with attentive resignation.

"I can hear them. They're—"

"Doesn't matter. Reality might be boring. Now watch and pretend my voice is hers, all right?" I shifted my tone to a grumpy hiss.

"Are you sure the giant we hired as a babysitter knows that term is metaphorical? Well? Are you? Answer me right now and answer me right, because I swear if I find out my husband has glamoured someone to come in his place so he can play fantasy Quidditch with his idiot friends while we're paying someone else to sit on the kids, I'm going to—"

"We don't have fantasy Quidditch," Ronan pointed out. But his tone was markedly lighter.

I did another one. Pointing out a resplendent fae gentleman standing near the food but not touching anything. "He's thinking, 'Gee, I wish those appetizers didn't give me explosive diarrhea. There's only so much glamour one can do to hide a crap stain.'"

Ronan snorted before he could stop himself. "Hey, lay off the glamour jokes."

"Fine. You do one then."

He scanned the gathering and drew my attention to a giant spider dancing with a three-tailed fox or kitsune that stood upright on its hind limbs.

"The spider's thinking: left foot, left foot, no *other* left foot. Buzz it all. Why don't they make dances more accessible to species with a superior number of legs? I'd like to see these dimwits dance the eight-step."

I snickered in a way most unsuited to my elegant dress. "You're a natural. Now come on, show me what food I can eat without soiling myself later."

Everything I tasted was incredible, and the pixie pomegranate cider was the perfect palette cleanser between bites. But there was plenty I wasn't game to taste either. A cutesy chubby creature waddling past us recommended, "Try the fried bark cannoli. It's divine." I held back when Ronan warned it would give me hallucinations for a week.

"So," I said, popping another heavenly morsel into my mouth and letting the flavors melt over my tongue. A beautiful fae woman shot me a poisonous glare. "Any jilted lovers I need to be concerned about?"

"Thousands."

"Is that all? In that case, I'll have another cake thingy. And I might need to borrow some of your armor to protect my back."

Strike appeared out of nowhere, and I nearly inhaled my cake thingy instead of swallowing it. "I'll guard your back. But I'm beginning to think you lied when you claimed you don't usually eat sugary foods for dinner."

"Even if that were true," I told her primly, "for however long this protection gig lasts, *you're* far more likely to give me a heart attack than clogged arteries."

Ronan tipped back the rest of his own cider. "Incoming."

I had a moment to second-guess all the food I'd just scoffed while I took in the two figures sweeping toward us.

They were evidently a matched set. The male fae's exquisite golden armor with black accents and distinctive shoulder plates that were reminiscent of leaves was echoed in the female's getup. An elegant black gown embellished with golden stitching and complex jewelry across her collarbone and shoulders that seemed more art than accessory. Like Ronan, they both had magnifi-cent wings, though the male's were a rich russet rather than onyx black.

Their faces were fearsomely lovely and impossible to read.

In contrast to the near-immortal vampires whose lifespan could last up to a millennium, fae did not live a great deal longer than humankind—topping out at about a hundred and fifty years. But their connection with Faerie meant they aged almost imperceptibly after adulthood—the magic ensuring their cells reproduced very near perfectly for every one of their hundred and some years—so their functional lifespan was effectively far longer.

Then, sometime in their second century at a moment no one could predict and for reasons no one fully understood, their connection with Faerie would abruptly sever, like a healthy limb being dropped by the tree. And in a handspan of days, their vitality would ebb to nothing and they'd pass away.

All of which meant I had no idea how old the fae approaching us might be. Because they looked, like Ronan and every fae I'd seen did, between twenty-five and thirty-five.

"Lyra, meet my parents. Count and Countess Nightwing of the Nightland district."

Count and Countess Nightwing of the Nightland district studied me like I was an oozing slug their five-year-old had just brought into the house and announced as his new pet.

"Um, nice to meet you," I said eloquently, uncertain what fae customs dictated as far as handshakes or courtly gestures went.

His mother's gaze landed back on Ronan. "It's been a long time since our bloodline has chosen to bed a human. How... quaint."

To my dismay, his father's gaze was still on me. He raised a dark, quizzical eyebrow. "How *did* you catch my son's interest?"

I kept my mouth shut. I'd figured out within a few seconds that none of this conversation was actually about me.

His gray eyes turned even colder as they shifted to his son. "Or is this merely another one of your subversive acts designed to throw insult at us and your ancestors?"

Ronan returned his glass to the table harder than necessary. "Despite what you choose to believe, my actions have never been centered around their impact on you. Disagreeing on core values and acting accordingly is *not* the same as defiance."

His father's expression didn't alter. "Do you expect us to believe it was coincidence that an undistinguished human girl captured your heart a week before the most public event of the year? Bad enough that you exploit tradition to invite a *vampire* into Faerie. But at least the vampire had the good sense to stay out of sight."

Ronan's dark eyes flashed, his anger hot against his father's ice, and I realized I'd never seen him angry before. Upset, half-dead, despairing, and hopeful, but never hot anger.

Until now.

"This *human girl* single-handedly saved hundreds of thousands of lives and the reputation of the fae a few weeks ago. By what right do you disparage her? What service have you rendered to the world recently? Or have you merely rested on the deeds of our ancestors?"

"That's strange," his mother said in a voice that was deceptively light. "*I* heard she was thrown in prison, miraculously managed to escape with the Hale brat, and almost killed two guards in the process."

Cold snaked down my spine.

But it wasn't the icy scorn from Ronan's parents that caused it and the goose bumps breaking out across my skin. As belittling as Lady and Lord Nightwing were, I'd seen their type before across a multitude of species. The inflated self-worth. The superior attitude. The immovable certainty of their own rightness. They couldn't shake the years Miles had put into teaching me how little species or heritage defined us compared to the choices we made. And my job had shown me often how believing yourself better than others was the first step to a host of evils.

So no, the cold fear and dread swamping my senses and fusing my spine into an immovable Popsicle was not emanating from Ronan's parents.

"Come now, Ronan," his mother was saying. "Dallying with criminals and human bedmates is fine for some, but *you* have a duty to your bloodline and the throne to uphold."

"I have never shied from my duty," Ronan said stiffly. "Only your definition of it."

I thought he'd made a solid point, but it was clear the words didn't even penetrate his parents' walls. They'd barely penetrated my own understanding as the cold grew deeper, filling my brain with fog.

I forced my ice-fused spine to bend, to turn. It was so cold, so brittle, I worried it would splinter.

An incorporeal being was drifting toward us. Shadowy mists endlessly shifting to form a vaguely humanoid figure. One rendered by a coy impressionist artist so that you might never make out the details of the face.

The chill grew worse the closer the being came, radiating waves of foreboding so great that I would've fled if I hadn't been frozen in place.

Ronan placed a steadying hand on my back. A beacon of warmth in the bitter cold.

Then the being spoke. "You must be Lyra," it said in a warm, kindly voice. "It's so lovely to meet you at last."

I managed to tear my gaze from the being's morphing features to stare at Ronan.

He looked relaxed. Relieved even.

The sight helped me find enough moisture in my mouth to reply.

"H-hi."

"Lyra, this is my dear friend and former tutor and bodyguard, Fallaas." Ronan leaned close to my ear and added, "They're a dread wight. A very good companion to have around, so long as they're on your side."

Whether or not Fallaas heard this addendum, they addressed Ronan's parents. "Forgive me for interrupting, but I simply had to meet the woman responsible for saving our boy's life here while he was in the outer world."

And like magic, Ronan's parents made their excuses and departed.

I thought I caught a suggestion of a smile in the shifting shadows of Fallaas's face. There was certainly the suggestion of a smile on Ronan's. And although I was still freezing and could feel the waves of bone-chilling dread emanating from them, I was no longer afraid.

Much.

"Thank you for the rescue," I said.

"Thank you for showing Ronan that sometimes it's okay to need rescuing," they replied.

Ronan winced.

"Besides, I really did want to meet you. I hope you won't allow those less gracious than yourself to steal your enjoyment of this beautiful evening."

I smiled—genuinely this time. "That *would* be a poor way to repay your kindness."

Fallaas inclined their shadowy visage in acknowledgment. "Well, duty calls. My kids will wail like banshees if I don't go and play with them as I promised, but it was lovely to make your acquaintance. And no matter what Lord Ronan there tells you, I've never seen him smile this much at an obligatory event in all the years I've known him. That alone tells me you're worth knowing."

Feeling began trickling back into my extremities as the dread wight drew away from us.

I glanced at Ronan.

"So… your parents. Are they always like that? That was only five times worse than I was thinking by the way."

Ronan snorted, then visibly forced himself to let go of his tension.

"The truth is, we want the same things. We just don't agree on how to go about it. They're convinced that what best serves Faerie happens to be what best serves themselves. To maintain power among the fae and the royal line, to keep the power among the old families. I believe what best serves Faerie is to serve all the beings within Faerie." He paused. "Perhaps they're right. Only time will tell."

His gaze picked out his parents from among the crowd, and I wasn't certain he was still talking to me when he went on.

"When the old ways are crumbling beneath you, you can cling to the fracturing foundation with every bit of your strength in the hopes you can shore it up a little longer—or you can let go and jump. Neither is safe. And fear can make fools of us all."

My interest was piqued, and I would've been happy to listen to him expand on the topic. But as if his parents' approach had given everyone else permission, another pair of fae were approaching in Fallaas's wake— even before the temperature had returned to the warm evening I remembered.

Ronan's attention snapped to them.

"Incoming," he growled. "Will you escape with me onto the dance floor?"

"I can't."

"Can't or won't?"

"I'd prefer to be fed on by a flotilla of piranha pixies."

His eyes sparkled. "I'm sure your dancing has to be better than my small talk."

And because of that sparkle, I caved.

"Fine." I released a put-upon sigh. "But don't blame me if I step on your toes."

And although I felt not unlike the spider with four left feet, we danced to avoid unwanted conversation until the stars had wheeled about in the sky and my cheap heel snapped.

"I wasn't expecting door-to-door service," I told Ronan as he escorted me up to my apartment.

"You're drunk on pixie cider, and you were having difficulty walking in those heels *before* one was broken."

I nodded gravely. "Fair point."

Though he'd fixed the heel as good as new moments after I'd snapped it.

We made it to my door and I stopped, turning to face him. He was closer than I expected. "Would you believe I actually had a fun time tonight?"

Ronan's lips quirked into a crooked smile. "I'll admit it was more entertaining than usual with you and your drone for company. Perhaps you could accompany me next year too?"

I stared, uncertain whether he was serious about that last part. Damn, he was gorgeous in his well-fitted armor. Grave and glorious like some heroic defender of old. And my experience to date had demonstrated he had the character to match.

"Perhaps I'll consider it," I agreed lightly.

He hadn't stepped back, so we were still standing close. Tantalizingly close. And those darn wings were on full display.

Maybe it was the cider, but he seemed to be watching me with equal intensity. His eyes flicked to my lips.

Was he thinking about kissing me?

My imagination grabbed that thought and dove deep. I'd accumulated plenty of accidental fantasies for it to draw on, and a delightful shiver rippled over my skin. I didn't even care that Strike might watch the show with the same curiosity she dedicated to all new experiences.

I leaned closer, just a little. Or was it him who'd moved?

Should I invite him in? What time was it? What time did I have to get up for work tomorrow? And who gave a crap about any of that stuff when I might be about to taste the man before me?

Then a new thought, a new desire, slipped into my mind.

Get rid of him. Fast.

The familiar helplessness of having my mind usurped snapped me out of my lurid imaginings faster than if Strike had started asking questions about human-fae anatomical compatibility. And with it, every ounce of surreal pleasure and peace I'd gleaned from the evening turned to ash in my mouth.

I leaped away from Ronan so fast my back hit the door. "Thanks again. See you around sometime, okay?"

Any intensity in his gaze that may or may not have been there snuffed out. Replaced by something else that vanished just as quickly.

I felt my face crease in a false smile. "Sorry to be abrupt, just busting for the bathroom, you know?" I crossed my legs together to provide credence to my excuse, then realized he probably couldn't see what my legs were doing under the floor-length dress.

"Of course. Good night, Lyra." He nodded toward my drone. "Strike."

Then he turned and departed down the hallway.

I watched him go, wishing with every unbroken part of me that I could leave with him. Instead, I opened the door to my apartment and the vicious nightmare of my reality waiting inside.

CHAPTER TWENTY-FOUR

For the second time in as many days, I was wearing heels. But this time it was at the bidding of the man I most hated and feared—instead of a hot and cranky fae doing me a giant favor. And the purpose for wearing those heels was entirely different too.

My visit to Faerie had been to keep my family safe.

My presence at the airport was to set events in motion that would leave millions, maybe billions, dead.

Metcalf's visit had been brief. Just long enough to ensure I'd do what he wanted today.

I hadn't slept after he'd left. Only stared at the blackened ceiling and prayed that somehow, someone or something would stop me from carrying out my orders.

Now I was at the airport after calling in sick to work, and it was clear my prayers had not been answered.

I stood on the tarmac where I should not have been,

accompanied by my drone that I should not have had, and longed to go back to traffic duty with every uncorrupted fiber of my being.

The prime minister of the United Kingdom's flight came in on schedule.

I'd expected to see a small private plane. The kind they always showed the rich elite stepping out of in movies. But that was foolish. Heads of state did not travel with just a few selected security guards. Heads of state traveled with enough security and staff to warrant a converted midsized commercial passenger aircraft.

Security personnel in black suits—almost entirely men—spilled out of the plane onto the tarmac in a seemingly endless wave. The airport officials had already been compelled to ignore me, so my attention was wholly on the arriving party.

I waited at a distance until my target—the prime minister of the United Kingdom—exited the plane through the same doorway as everyone else. He was inconsiderately wearing a navy suit so dark that it was almost indistinguishable from afar, but I caught a glimpse of his face as he descended the steps amid more black suits, and that was all I needed.

I strolled forward, my pace neither fast nor slow, my heels clicking against the tarmac in a subliminal, age-old signal that told all those armed and suited men that I was not a threat.

They couldn't know how wrong they were. Couldn't know that before I began my approach, I'd winked out of existence on all the security feeds. That what I was about to do wouldn't be recorded in anything but the history books.

If there was anyone left to write them.

Strike watched unobtrusively from the shadowed nook I'd been waiting in. It had been a simple matter to compel the airport staff to allow her entrance. But there was no need to heighten the concerns of the prime minister's security personnel and make my job harder by having the drone follow me now.

There were at least sixty people there, and at least half a dozen of them would have the latest in magic and threat-detection tech. Too many people to simultaneously brainwash with any finesse.

But all I needed to do was dissuade them from shooting me for just long enough for me to draw a little nearer. Just long enough for me to reach the mind of the prime minister.

Stand down, I ordered the foremost suits. *Pretend you recognize me. You want me to come closer.* I nabbed the closest six-foot wall of muscle. *Escort me to the prime minister.*

Hands twitched toward guns and away again. Questions were murmured into earpieces, but no alarms were raised.

And just like that, the ocean of black suits parted around me like Moses and the Red Sea.

A small, stupid part of me even enjoyed it.

The prime minister's head turned in surprise.

"What's going on?" he barked. But then I was close enough to him too. *Greet me like you recognize me. You want to talk to me. Tell your security it's okay.*

His face tightened and then broke into a smile. The hand he'd been raising in protest or command turned into a wave of greeting.

His security detail immediately relaxed, and most of them turned their attention outward again, scanning for possible threats.

And then I was talking to the prime minister.

My tongue went over the rehearsed script, welcoming him to Las Vegas and informing him of the local police who would be liaising with his personal protection detail as he traveled to his hotel.

All the while, my mind wielded Metcalf's magic in an altogether different agenda.

Without a word of it passing my lips, I compelled him to go home after the summit and prepare his national security forces for war. To convince them there was a credible threat, that multiple nuclear states were moving—plotting imminent and undeclared war against them and their allies. To ready their defenses, their people, their long-range weapons. Tell them that this was not a drill, that when the missile approach warning systems lit up, when Washington was destroyed as the opening move by the enemy, it would not be a glitch, a cyberattack, a computer error. It would be the end of the world as they knew it, and they had better be ready.

Color drained from the prime minister's face as the

real message sank in. His dark navy suit suddenly making his skin look bloodless and sickly instead of just his usual pasty white.

Now nod and smile and say goodbye, I ordered.

The prime minister did so, and I strolled away at the same pace I'd come.

I'm unremarkable, I pushed at his security detail as I left. *Forgettable. You don't feel the need to talk to anyone about me.* The weak compulsion wouldn't last forever, but by the time anyone thought to look, I'd be long gone, and the camera footage would show only my shadow falling across the tarmac.

One down.

I crossed the UK prime minister off my mental checklist and retreated to my corner of the airport to await the next arrival.

Because this was what Metcalf wanted.

Nuclear war.

It shouldn't have been possible. And yet it was. Metcalf had crowed about how the whole world was so focused on controlling people with too much magical power that they'd overlooked how, for an entire century, the president of the United States had single-handedly held the power to wipe out most of the human race. Had carried that power with him or her everywhere in the form of a clunky black suitcase and a card with a code.

When you thought about any one person possessing a power like that, it was a miracle the world hadn't already ended. Yet for nearly a hundred years after the nuclear arms race between the United States and Soviet Union heated up, the deterrence of mutually assured destruction had held.

It was especially miraculous given the very real risk of accidental launches, tech glitches, and human error— and that was before you even got to human intention. But it had held nevertheless.

Now, the devil was going to bring that miraculous streak to an end.

Despite a century of disarmament initiatives, promises, treaties, and politics, there were still approximately ten thousand nukes floating about the planet, with around a third of those on high alert status, ready to go.

Even a few dozen nukes could slaughter untold millions. Not just those who were torn apart or burned alive in the initial blast—but those who would die of their injuries, of acute radiation poisoning, of lack of aid, and farther afield, from contaminated water sources and cancers caused by radioactive fallout... The list went on.

Detonate a mere hundred even modest nukes no larger than the one dropped on Hiroshima, and the resulting ash cloud would block out the sun over entire continents and take several years to disperse— potentially resulting in a nuclear winter affecting billions.

There were no test runs for the end of the world.

No one knew for sure what would happen to the survivors.

But everyone agreed it would be bad.

And it would be even worse because Metcalf would still be alive and no doubt had plans to use those survivors for his own ends.

I hated to think what the psychopath could do in the power vacuum left behind by the world's governments destroying each other.

Because as much as nuclear war was a gamble, a roll of the dice for a man who liked to have everyone under his control, Metcalf was too smart and too self-serving not to have a plan for his own safety and prosperity. Magic would help the survivors recover and make sure he wasn't too inconvenienced. And as Metcalf had smugly pointed out, it would certainly give the world more important things to do than hunting him down.

Of course, brainwashing the world's leaders alone might not have been enough to guarantee nuclear war. To push these nations toward mutually assured destruction. The majority of nuclear states had multiple layers of safeguards in place: "no first strike" policies, group consensus required to sign off on any nuclear launches, and other useful precautions. It was even remotely possible that if the president of the United States ordered nuclear strikes that seemed to come out of nowhere, someone down the very short chain of command might be brave enough to stop and question them.

That was what Washington was for.

Metcalf didn't like leaving anything to chance.

Somehow, sometime soon, he was going to drop a thermonuclear warhead on Washington, DC.

That reprehensible act would convince the world the threat was real. Convince those who mattered that the intel was credible.

As indescribable horror rained down on America's capital city, the skeptics would become believers.

And Metcalf's plan didn't need to work flawlessly. It didn't even need to work well. So long as one single person managed to launch one single nuke, snap decisions would be made by terrified, furious, fallible leaders all over the world under unimaginable pressure, and the devil might just succeed in bringing hell to earth.

The devil and I, that is.

Eight hours later, I'd had similar interactions with four presidents, one chancellor, one king, and three more prime ministers. And the sentiment stone I'd used to compel them was worn down to nothing more than grit in my pocket.

I knew Metcalf had covered the other world leaders, including the US president, who had been arriving for the summit via different airports. It was no wonder he'd needed a second person wielding his magic to pull this off. Even if the schedules and locations hadn't conflicted, there was no way he could have compelled so many today on his own.

I left my assigned battleground and headed home.

My stride was relaxed even though my feet ached from the shoes. But my heart had never been heavier.

It had been so easy.

So terrifyingly easy.

Metcalf and I had just changed the fate of the world. And no one had even noticed.

All this time I'd been wishing, hoping, *praying* one of my friends would realize something was wrong despite my hateful attempts to hide it and come to my rescue. Or that someone would figure out what Metcalf was up to—independent of my involvement—and manage to put a stop to it. That against all odds, I would be able to use Metcalf's interest in me, use the horrifying things I'd done and learned under Metcalf's control, to take him down. Perhaps even use his own magic—the magic he'd foisted on me—against him.

But after what I'd just pulled off, I didn't have it in me to hope anymore.

In a few days' time, unimaginable hell would rage across the earth.

And only Metcalf had the power to stop it.

CHAPTER TWENTY-FIVE

I headed home to pack. Metcalf had ordered me to meet at his chosen rendezvous—Devil's Hole—at dusk. Where we would apparently be flying out to a safe and secret location so he could "sit back and drink champagne while the world self-destructs."

I didn't want to pack. I wanted to hit something.

Instead, I wondered whether Strike would be allowed to come with me. I'd grown strangely attached to the overly curious, emotionally *un*supportive, anti-ice-cream drone over the past few days. Probably because she was the only one who knew everything I'd gone through since Metcalf had set me in his sights, and —wherever the devil was taking me—she was the closest thing to a friendly face I was likely to get.

Maybe I *should* have invested in an emotional support drone.

Even without the heels, it would've been too hot to

jog in the height of the afternoon, but I was feeling an extreme aversion to cab rides. So I located one of the city's e-scooters and made my weary way home to do Metcalf's bidding.

Outside my apartment building, a familiar figure leaning against a black G-Class Mercedes almost made me run my scooter into a street sign.

"Dad? What are you doing here?"

His beloved blue gaze searched my face. "The kids are still in Faerie, sweetheart. I just wanted to see you with my own eyes and make sure you're okay."

Tears welled, but the Metcalf parasite refused to let them fall.

Miles opened his arms in invitation, and I rushed into them. Acutely aware that this might be the last time I ever saw him. Ever felt his arms around me in that carefully gentle embrace that was the first place I'd ever felt secure.

But damn was I grateful for this last time.

I stayed there, wrapped in his warmth and love, for as long as the compulsion would allow me. Then withdrew, bracing my knees against their sudden weakness. Opening my mouth to lie and tell him I was fine. That he should get back to Faerie. At least the parasite and I could agree on that last point.

That was when Miles *moved*. At full vampiric speed. And I heard and felt the snap of metal around my wrists before I could process that he'd just handcuffed me. With anti-magic handcuffs. And before I could even begin to react to that, he bundled me into the car he'd been leaning against and slammed the door.

The engine revved to life. And I caught a glimpse of Ronan in the driver's seat.

What on earth was—?

"We've got you now, darling," Dad said. "We won't let him hurt you anymore."

Tears stung my eyes again, but the compulsions won out over my real emotions.

"Who? What's going on? I need to be at work…"

Miles looked at me with something like pity in his gaze.

"We *know*, Lyra. Your friend Stewie was worried about you and didn't trust the authorities to protect you from Metcalf. So, once he got out, he took it upon himself to keep an ear on you from time to time. From a safe distance of course. And last night he overheard Metcalf paying you a visit."

I swallowed hard, deeply touched by Stewie's concern and paranoid tendencies that drove him to look out for me. Too late. But even still.

The parasite was *not* touched—urging me to bide my time, find out what they knew, then make a break for it at any cost.

"Aurelis has been liaising with your drone's creator and confirmed that Strike records any activity involving a third party and keeps it for thirty days to establish grounds for lawful self-defense if called for. The data is impossible to hack into externally and has self-destruction safeguards if it's tampered with. But Zax put some code together along with her proprietary override, so Aurelis will be able to access the footage shortly."

I only noticed then that Strike must have followed me into the car and was now sitting on the front passenger seat, as complacent as could be. Ronan had plugged something into her, probably beginning the override procedure.

It appeared the drone had decided Miles abducting me wasn't a threat, and I was abruptly glad for her hundred and one questions about my family.

I was also glad I'd changed her protocols not to intervene unless I had a weapon aimed at me—just in case her suspicious and bloodthirsty nature prompted her to act regardless.

But geez. The footage.

Aurelis, Dad, and Ronan would see me pick up that garrote. Would see—

"So you don't need to talk," my father continued. "Just rest as much as his compulsions allow until we can figure out a way to free you. Or else wait for his magic to wear off naturally in another week or so. Either way, we'll keep you out of his reach. You're safe now."

Safe.

My body convulsed like I was under one of Strike's lightning attacks. That was unacceptable. Metcalf needed me.

No.

But their help had come too late. I'd already done

234

the unthinkable. And I needed to act against Metcalf before he brought about the end of the world.

Whichever desire was riding me, I had to get out of here.

"No." My head was shaking like Miles couldn't understand my words. "No. I can't stay here. I have to go right now."

Pain flickered across my father's face.

"I'm sorry, Lyra. I think it's best you rest now until you're in a more secure location."

Then he *moved* again. A delicate mist touched my nose, my lips, and for a fleeting moment, my panic subsided. I slid into drugged slumber.

CHAPTER TWENTY-SIX

I woke up in a prison cell.

A familiar prison cell.

A *Faerie* prison cell.

Which in actual fact was more like a hotel room, but I knew just how hard it was to escape from.

I bolted upright. What time was it? I had to meet Metcalf at Devil's Hole.

A wave of dizziness made me lie back down. And as I did, I realized someone was talking. Someone I couldn't see.

But I didn't need to see them to identify them.

"Thunderation. I thought once she was here she'd be safe. That we could hand the footage over to the authorities and focus on her well-being."

It was Miles's voice. And he only fell back on antiquated curses when he was particularly upset.

"We thought so too." That was Ronan. "But the footage proves Aurelis is right. Lyra's our best hope of capturing Metcalf without a bloodbath, and possibly the world's *only* hope for extracting the information we need to prevent the catalyst of nuclear war. If he's killed or escapes or cannot be made to talk, the consequences will be unfathomable."

"I'm always right," Aurelis put in helpfully.

"Perhaps," Dad conceded, his words tired and heavy. "But this discussion is pointless if we can't free her from the compulsions."

I belatedly recalled the weird glamour trick that hid the cell bars behind a nonexistent wall to give you the illusion of privacy. Since Metcalf's parasite didn't prevent me from wanting to see their faces, I pushed myself into a sitting position more slowly this time and flopped my legs—which were acting more like wet noodles than limbs—over the side of the bed. Then I dragged my weary body toward the voices, using one of the walls that actually existed for support.

Ronan might have been the first to notice. Or at least he was the first to talk. "Lyra. We know you can't contribute to this conversation as yourself right now. But we thought we'd talk here so the part of you that's still you can be aware of what's happening."

The illusion of the wall faded away, and I could see them all. Aurelis. Ronan. Strike. And my dad. Whose gaze fixed on me like a starving man offered poisoned food.

I could imagine all too clearly how that would tickle Metcalf.

"She's been through hell," Dad murmured, still transfixed. "She needs safety and therapy, not getting thrust straight back into it."

Aurelis huffed. "Are you telling me she wouldn't choose to throw herself into this if she was in her right mind?"

Miles didn't answer straightaway, and when he did, his voice was subdued. "No. You're right. I just… Did you see what he did to her? Do you know how deeply that will cut at her soul? I don't want to send her back into that monster's reach."

Even Aurelis was wise enough not to be dismissive this time. "I saw. But she's tougher than she looks."

My father pressed his fingers to the bridge of his nose. "How would we attempt to break the compulsion?"

Aurelis flicked her wings. "Well, we know anti-magic doesn't work, or handcuffs would be all we needed. Theorists believe magic of this nature changes the neural pathways in the brain, which is why even after Metcalf is out of range of his victim, the compulsions hold strong."

Ronan frowned. "There's a fae healing tonic I was planning on giving her that might speed up the dissolution of the unnatural pathways. But even assuming it works, that would still mean a few days, not under an hour."

"What if you give her a dozen of those tonics?" Aurelis half joked.

"Her body would go into overdrive and kill itself attempting to regenerate."

"Ah. Let's not do that then." She considered for a moment. "It's been hypothesized that the hive mind some species share would prevent mental manipulation. But I'm not sure how we could connect Lyra's mind into one or whether it would work after the fact. Or what side effects there might be…"

Strike spoke for the first time since I'd woken. "Why don't you do a memory wipe and return her to factory settings?"

Ronan shook his head. "Humans don't—"

"Wait," Aurelis interrupted. "Could that work? If a vampire wipes someone's memory of being compelled, would it also wipe any neural pathway changes that compulsion created?"

"I don't believe it's been tried," Miles replied. "But with good reason. Vampires can only affect memories from the last ten minutes or so. Just enough for the person we just drank from to wonder why they're feeling light-headed. And we can't be selective about which memories we wipe either. Lyra's been brainwashed by Metcalf for eight days."

Ronan cleared his throat uncomfortably. "Actually, if you feed from me first, eight days of memory loss might be achievable."

Miles blanched. "You're willing to lay your life in my hands? Your people would kill me."

What Ronan was suggesting was utterly taboo.

"You'd have my consent. Technically there are no laws against it."

"You cannot trust me that much."

"I took a leap of faith in your daughter and did not regret it. This time there are even more lives at stake."

Miles shook his head slowly. "I noticed the new generation of fae is different, but I had no idea how much." He paused. Swallowed. "Even if we were both willing, I don't know. Is it justifiable to wipe her memories without giving her any say in the matter?"

Ronan rubbed the back of his neck, perhaps already imagining my father's fangs sinking into his carotid artery. "Would *you* want to remember what she's been through? We won't hide what happened from her, but a layer of disconnect in this case could be a good thing."

"I'd gladly forget a week of my life to take this bastard down," Aurelis growled.

Given my dragon partner's love of knowledge, that proclamation was more fierce than it sounded.

The parasite was listening closely, all but vibrating with anger and the need to do something—anything— to get to my master.

The rest of me was with Aurelis on this one.

She was right of course. Metcalf had to be stopped at any price. And Ronan was once more willing to lay his neck on the line.

How could I do any less?

Ronan rested a hand on Dad's shoulder. "She's too old to need a guardian, but I think the decision should be up to you, Miles. I've witnessed enough of her character that I think I know what choice she'd make. But you're the person who knows her best."

My father stared at me where I was being supported by the wall, his gaze anguished. Then he bowed his head.

I blinked. And was suddenly somewhere else. Somewhere I had the misfortune to recognize as a prison cell. And Miles was hovering anxiously over me, his eyes shifting from memory-wiping burgundy back to their usual blue.

My head ached, and my body felt like it had been used as a trampoline by my younger siblings. Or maybe stampeded over by a herd of giant centipedes sporting hobnail boots. What the heck? Had I been drinking? Had I been in an accident? What on earth was going on?

"Dad?" I croaked. "What happened? Where are we? The last thing I remember is…" I shut my mouth when I recalled I hadn't actually told him about that yet.

Wait. He was supposed to be in Faerie, wasn't he? But not the prison—

"What do you remember, darling?" His long, gentle fingers brushed over my forehead the way they used to when he'd tucked me into my childhood bed each night.

"You… you need protection. We think Metcalf is coming after me."

"Yes." He nodded like this was old news.

Maybe it was old news.

"What happened? What day is it?"

Dad's face was pinched with concern.

"Do you trust me, sweetheart?"

I sat upright in alarm. "Yes. With my life. What's wrong?"

"You're safe, darling. We're all safe for now. But I need to tell you some things. Serious things… And we don't have much time if we want to stay that way."

CHAPTER TWENTY-SEVEN

Tears, hot and shameful, poured down my cheeks as I watched the footage Strike had stored in her memory.

Metcalf offering me his power and patting me on the head like his obedient dog.

Me, forcing a redheaded woman to slap herself.

Me, forcing a room full of people to turn on each other in savage desperation.

Me, walking up to an injured young man with a garrote dangling from my fingers. The terror on his face as I approached. His lack of thrashing as I'd compelled him to stillness while my abruptly invisible hands took his life.

Horror. Disbelief. Anguish. Denial. Shame. *More* hot shame. Revulsion. And the dirty feeling of being irreversibly violated.

The first thing I did was stagger to the bathroom to empty my stomach's contents. Like I'd apparently done after I'd made that fae woman slap herself and seen the hatred in her eyes.

But I didn't have time to be sick or punish myself.

Because those things weren't even the worst I'd done.

Because the fruits of the worst I'd done were still to come.

Strike had recorded Metcalf's instructions to me beforehand. And she'd recorded me as I'd walked up to one head of state after another, winking out of the camera screen, but visible by the bodies parting around me. The shock then dumb obedience on the world leaders' faces. The shadow on the tarmac.

But—and it was a very *big* but—my mind was my own again. No longer under Metcalf's control. And while fear had shriveled my gut into a cold, hard stone, righteous anger burned hotter and brighter.

I was going to take that son of a bitch down.

CHAPTER TWENTY-EIGHT

Minutes later, we were climbing into Ronan's car at Faerie border control and speeding through a gateway out onto a dark and deserted desert road near Death Valley Junction and the Nevada and California border, Aurelis flying fast and low behind us.

I hadn't even known car travel was possible through the gateways.

Three miles out, Ronan, Miles, and Aurelis joined the waiting incursion force that would spring into action if (and when) I failed. And I continued on alone.

Well, alone except for the drone that had been at my side for the past nine days, but I had little memory of beyond her judgy stance on ice cream.

I'd seen plenty of *her* "memories" of me and Metcalf though. None of them good.

Which meant I had some idea of what would be waiting for me.

Colton Metcalf, the fae woman Ronan had identified as Neyomara Mistweaver, a trader who'd been on a routine acquisition run when Metcalf had bound her to him, and nineteen others chosen for their magic abilities and brainwashed to protect the enemy.

Nineteen others instead of twenty because I'd choked the life from one to steal his magic.

Maybe eighteen if Metcalf had left the rich tourist in Vegas.

Victims. Hostages. Lethal opponents.

They were a big part of why I was going in alone. Them and every other person Metcalf's magic would grab and turn against their own side in an incursion situation.

I would attempt to stop the bloodbath before it began.

Miles and my friends hadn't exactly been happy about the alone part, but it was impossible to deny the sense of it. The only thing we'd lose from trying this way first was a few tense minutes.

The other—and primary—reason I was going in alone was because if Metcalf was killed or managed to escape during the aforementioned bloodbath, Washington, DC, would be destroyed by an unknown party, heralding in nuclear war.

Even knowing what Metcalf had set in motion, there could be no stopping it unless we could prevent the trigger from ever taking place. Compelled as they were, the heads of state could not be reasoned with. They could possibly be detained, but detaining them alone might not be enough. And to attempt to stop them from contacting their national security forces would start an international incident by itself.

We had to prevent Washington, DC, from falling to a thermonuclear attack at any price.

And to do it, we needed Metcalf.

Or more specifically, we needed his knowledge of where the attack was coming from.

With the bastard unaware his week of brainwashing had been undone, I should be able to stroll straight through all his security measures and walk right up to him. And if I could get close enough to fill a new sentiment stone with his magic, then neutralize his own power with handcuffs, I could single-handedly force the information we needed from him.

With luck, I'd also be able to override the compulsions he'd forced on everyone there—before anyone unwillingly killed anyone.

The logic was sound.

But the fear of facing him again, at risking doing unspeakable things under his control again, made me want to flee back to that prison cell, curl up in a ball, and wait till it was over.

So I drew on the simmering rage to keep my hands steady on the wheel as the headlights lit up the group of people gathered around the otherwise abandoned tourist destination. The group of people protecting Metcalf with their bodies and magic. And the chopper towering over all of them, ready to whisk Metcalf and his chosen lackeys off to an unknown location.

My number one priority was to find out how to stop Washington from being nuked and therefore prevent the end of the world before it began.

My second priority was to rescue the civilians Metcalf was using as both hostages and his personal bodyguards.

Both of those objectives would require my possession of Metcalf's magic. Which meant I had to get close enough to touch him.

Only then, coming in maddening third place, could I turn my attention to taking the asshole down. No matter how much the part of me that wasn't petrified wanted to make him pay.

I drew on that rage again to shore up my resolve as I switched off the headlights and climbed out of the car.

In minutes, this whole thing would be over. And chances were that one or both of us would be dead.

Hopefully Metcalf. But either way, I wouldn't spend too long under his control.

On my side, I had the chain magic and three sentiment stones. Two in my left pocket, one in my right. I'd considered bringing the fourth too, but I would already be juggling more magics than I'd ever attempted before.

The first stone was filled with the memory and

sensation of pyromancy magic that Metcalf had ordered me to draw from one of his selected hostages. Intended to aid in my escape "just in case" any of the G23 security forces had caught on to what was happening. The second stone I'd filled just minutes earlier with my father's supernatural speed.

The third and final stone was empty. Waiting for Metcalf's evil magic. Magic that made my skin crawl just thinking about it. Magic I dearly wished I'd never have to use again.

So I didn't think about it. Didn't think about anything except putting one foot in front of the other.

I did not care to tally up all the advantages Metcalf had on his side.

If only he'd been incautious enough to choose a rendezvous location where we could've turned the whole playing field into an anti-magic zone, I wouldn't have had to go in alone. But he was arrogant, not stupid. And he'd chosen Devil's Hole as a rendezvous not just for its name, but because it was one of the many areas within the Mojave Desert that defied the use of anti-magic on any significant scale.

As a result, the odds were stacked against me. Especially since I'd be trying to keep everyone alive, while he wouldn't hesitate to sacrifice any of us. Hell, he'd probably revel in it.

And he had Neyomara to protect him.

Ronan had warned that even outside Faerie, fae had

the capacity to shield two or maybe three people from magical attack. Chances were, Metcalf was smart enough to be using that protection, which meant the power contained in the sentiment stones wouldn't do me much good in a direct assault.

But the fae shielding didn't stop the person within from wielding their own magic—the silver lining of which was that my mimic magic worked too. We'd tested it to make sure.

So I turned my mind to Metcalf's weaknesses instead of his strengths.

He was unsuspecting. He was arrogant. And he would be magically fatigued. After planting compulsions in so many of the world's leaders today, he *should* be exhausted.

But so was I.

I could feel it in every leaden step as I picked my way over the dirt and rocks toward the impending confrontation. It wasn't just fear and dread making my legs heavy and slow to respond. I was battling fatigue too. Physical. Magical. And emotional.

Ronan had given me some sort of Faerie draught that had perked me up about ten times as much as a cup of coffee and apparently replenished my ability to use magic somewhat too. But it was my determination and the anger I was hanging on to with white-knuckled fists that were preventing me from crashing.

I kept walking, drawing closer. And then I was stepping into the circle of light provided by multiple lanterns, trying to keep all those emotions from my face. Then second-guessing myself. What had I looked like on all those forgotten occasions? I hadn't thought to pay attention to that detail in the video footage. Hadn't thought of anything much besides horror and shame.

"Ah, little lyrebird," Metcalf crooned, straightening up from amid his wall of live bodies. "You're late. I was beginning to think you weren't coming."

"Car troubles," I lied.

Metcalf waved a dismissive hand. "You overestimate my interest. Shut up while I concentrate."

His magic, forgotten and yet sinisterly familiar, wormed into my head, and my mouth clamped shut.

I stumbled as panic welled inside me, only his repugnant compulsion keeping me from screaming. From giving myself away.

Metcalf had bent back over whatever he'd been doing before I'd shown up, but my jerky misstep made his eyes flick to me. Not for long. Just enough to make my heart stop for a beat or three.

I drew in a deep breath—largely through my nose since my jaw wasn't working properly.

I didn't need to talk. I just had to get closer.

Strike had followed me out the car and hovered nearby as a silent witness. A silent witness relaying every detail to the incursion force standing by.

She'd been ordered not to intervene until I'd gotten the information from Metcalf. Not unless it was to stop me from dying—and even then only with nonlethal force.

She hadn't been pleased about that. For a drone that had been built for the sole purpose of protection, she seemed to have a bloodthirsty streak.

I took another slow step forward, my left hand clutching the unused sentiment stone in my pocket. Another shuffling step. My sudden stumble had drawn his eye, so I kept my movements steady, smooth, but without apparent purpose. Like I was drifting over to him almost by accident or bored curiosity.

What was he doing anyway?

I couldn't see what was on the ground, but if I'd had a gun, I would've had a clear shot to his head. Unfortunately, my mission wasn't that simple. Taking him down would not stop the events he and I had set in motion. And I hadn't brought any lethal weapons with me anyway unless you counted the magic in my pockets. The magic the fae woman was guarding him against. In fact, of the entire incursion team, only Strike possessed a traditionally lethal weapon. Because she was the only one Metcalf couldn't control.

Before he'd been apprehended the first time, one of Metcalf's favorite moves had been to compel arresting officers to use their guns against their comrades.

Putting each other out of action with Tasers was a whole lot better than shooting your teammates dead.

Besides, we were trying *not* to kill anyone.

The same could not be said for those Metcalf had

commandeered to guard him. And I was acutely aware of that fact as I passed the elderly woman with her gun that never missed. Passed the middle-aged man the records had identified as an aeromancer. And as I drew closer to the fae woman, Neyomara, who was, as ever, standing by Metcalf's side.

As soon as I acted against Metcalf, they would turn on me. Every one of them.

It was akin to trying to take down the bad guy and rescue the hostages. Only the hostages were more liable to shoot you than cooperate.

My mouth was so dry now that even if my tongue hadn't been compelled to muteness, I wouldn't have been able to speak.

But I was close. So close. And Metcalf wasn't paying me any attention.

This might be my chance. Only four feet separated us. Close enough to risk lunging at him…

Except he didn't need time to spin.

Didn't need time to physically react.

He could stop me with a thought.

And then the game was up. And I would have already lost.

Besides, if I could brush against him as if by accident, I might be able to fill the sentiment stone without him even noticing. And if I managed to pull that miracle off, maybe I could slap the cuffs taped to the small of my back on him before he realized what was happening.

Yeah right.

My palms were sweating. Sweat didn't interfere with sentiment stones, did it?

I drew in a deep breath and took another step. Another. And finally saw what it was that held Metcalf's attention.

A bomb.

At least, I figured that's what it was based on the bright red label that said *EXPLOSIVE* on the box he was fishing yellowish bricks out of. He was adding them to a sizable stack of the same bricks. A second smaller box held blasting caps—the more volatile detonators that would trigger the explosion of the more stable mass explosives. And by the look of the near-empty boxes, he was almost done.

My gut clenched. He was going to blow up everyone we left behind. Going to make them stand there like good obedient little sheep until the force of the blast tore them limb from limb.

How was I even surprised? I'd watched the footage of him telling me they'd all be dead soon anyway.

But Metcalf possessed a level of careless cruelty I just couldn't wrap my head around.

His attention jerked to me, and I flinched. But it was pleasure rather than suspicion that lit his face. "Just making sure we don't leave any witnesses," he said conversationally. "But which one of them should we get to set it off? The pyromancer perhaps? I did get the old traditional fuse caps just for fun. Or you could do it from the chopper once we're out of range…"

I felt the *shut up while I concentrate* compulsion wearing off. Or maybe he wanted me to answer and so made it possible.

Instead, I crossed the final distance between us as if on shocked autopilot and whispered, "I've never seen so many explosives before."

I reached out to touch the top yellowish block and "accidentally" brushed against his arm.

Metcalf's smile didn't waver.

The unique, ugly sensation of his power rushed into me, and I channeled it into the empty stone still hidden in my left pocket.

Then I gripped the stone beside it—the one I'd filled with the help of my dear father—and *moved*.

With my dad's vampiric speed, I yanked the handcuffs from the small of my back and snapped them around Metcalf's wrists.

Or one of his wrists. Because the fae woman had supernatural speed too. Her fist snapped out and struck me in the face.

I reeled back fast enough that she only split my lip instead of breaking my teeth and grappled for Metcalf's stone.

Idiot. I should have compelled Neyomara over to my side before making my move.

I dodged another whirlwind strike and reached for her mind. *Protect me*, I ordered. *Shield me from magic and guard my body against other threats. Try not to kill anyone.*

But it was Strike who zapped the senior weapon mage at the moment she pulled the trigger.

The fae's power protected against magical assault, but a magically augmented bullet was still a bullet. And even being zapped by Strike's lightning-like weapon, the weapon mage didn't *miss*.

The bullet entered my arm instead of my heart.

A shock wave of agony ricocheted through my left side, and for a moment, I couldn't think, couldn't move, couldn't do anything but brace myself against the pain.

Neyomara pivoted me out of the way of a charging attacker while a swarm of wraithlike hornets fizzled harmlessly against her shield.

Her shield that protected only me.

Like Metcalf, I couldn't tell her to protect herself from magic, because then she could protect herself from me. And until Metcalf and his bodyguards were dealt with, I needed her aid to keep me alive.

So I exploited her, just as he had, leaving her vulnerable.

Strike zapped two more of the attacking hostages with her lightning weapon.

Then my body unfroze.

My left hand still worked, and although curling my fingers around one of the sentiment stones sent a fresh wave of fiery pain through my side, I almost wept in relief that they moved at all.

I needed to compel Metcalf to tell me where the Washington threat was coming from, but I needed to survive first. So I shoved blindly at the minds around me, ordering them to *stop.*

That was when I learned it was a lot harder to override a repeatedly ingrained compulsion than it was someone's own will. Especially en masse. Or maybe I was more magicked out than I realized. Or maybe it was difficult to focus through the burning agony of my bullet wound.

Regardless, I only affected about half of the attacking hostages.

Fire lit up the night in my peripheral vision. Not knowing whether Neyomara's shield would hold against magic-called but mundane flames, I spun, fumbling for the pyromancy stone in my other pocket. The pyromancer's control stopped at the fae shield, but the fire kept going, licking at my face before the stone's magic rendered me impervious to the flames. I diverted them around Neyomara and into the sky where they wouldn't hurt anyone, then choked on the smell of my own singed eyebrows as a new fear seeped into my consciousness.

The explosives. So long as Metcalf was within the blast zone, no one should *intentionally* set them off. But this skirmish was a chaotic shit show that would only get messier.

Even so, I was in no position to do anything right now except try to stay alive.

Not letting go of the pyromancy stone, I flung out my good arm at a rushing hostage who'd figured out their magic wasn't going to work and dug out a knife instead.

My magical chain tangled in their legs and sent them sprawling, and I heated the handle of the knife to make sure they'd drop it in the dirt even as I sent my chain spinning toward the next threat. Neyomara was fighting off someone—several someones—behind me.

Trying to spare those attempting to kill us put us at a major disadvantage. And I didn't dare compel any other hostage to protect me for fear it would be a death sentence.

Backup was coming.

If Neyomara and I could survive long enough for it to arrive.

Sixty seconds was what Aurelis had promised. Surely we could hold on for however many remained…

Strike rained down lightning blast after lightning blast, temporarily taking the recipients out of action without causing mortal wounds. But there were so many. And she was under fire too.

A mage with the ability to duplicate himself made so many copies that he surrounded us. Every copy charged us at once with makeshift weapons, and I had no idea which, if any, was the original. I curled my fingers to grip Metcalf's stone again and compelled them all to *back off.*

It didn't work.

The duplicates must be immune to mind control. And while I was pretty sure I'd be shielded from them in turn, Neyomara wouldn't be. I wielded my chain magic like a stock whip to keep them back, aware they might only be a distraction for the true attack. But they ran straight into the lashing, bone-breaking links, heedless of doing damage to themselves. Frantically I searched for the original. Spotted him staring at us in concentration ten yards away, and shoved the compulsion at him directly. *Stop.*

The duplicates vaporized and streaked back into the mage, their weapons dropping harmlessly to the dirt.

That was when I realized my mistake.

In the frenzied imperative of staying alive, Metcalf, unnoticed, had managed to get his handcuff off. No doubt with the help of a brainwashed puppet I'd failed to subdue.

I found out when an aeromancer attack that Neyomara's shielding should've protected me from literally stole the air from my lungs.

Metcalf had compelled the fae woman back to his side.

Then I felt the beginning of a compulsion worming into my brain, and the horror of that overwhelmed even my panic at being unable to breathe.

Except something cut it off before it could take hold. And this time when I gasped for breath, my lungs filled with oxygen.

Two seconds later, I saw why.

Aurelis was speeding toward us, her familiar shape blocking out the stars. And in a gesture I did not under-value, she'd deigned to carry Ronan with her.

Ronan, who could shield me against magical attack like Neyomara had. Only since he was here of his own volition, he'd be able to shield himself too.

Ronan who would've been able to fly himself here mere seconds after Aurelis. But those seconds would've made all the difference in my becoming Metcalf's weapon once more.

Tears stung my eyes.

I knew Miles was coming in with the rest of the cavalry—prepared to reverse any fresh compulsions Metcalf placed on those in the incursion force. But what if I'd been under Metcalf's control when he arrived? What if I'd killed my dad while he tried to save me?

No... I couldn't think like that.

A fresh onslaught stopped me thinking of anything except the next few seconds.

My inexperience with someone else's magic had always made me less effective than its true owner. And Metcalf's mental compulsion was stronger and defter than mine. Five of the ten or so hostages I'd worked so hard to freeze in place were already moving again. Were trying to kill me again. And my friends were still too far away to help beyond what Ronan was already doing.

That was when Metcalf spotted Aurelis too.

When he recognized the powerful dragon as the greatest threat and focused nearly all his magic on her.

We'd anticipated that. But we hadn't known what effect it would have on a species known for its resistance to magic.

I saw Aurelis toss her head as if trying to shake off a particularly irksome bug before I yanked my gaze away. I had to make the most of the moments she bought.

Grabbing Metcalf's stone again, I focused my own coercion on Neyomara, thinking I might snatch her shielding from Metcalf while he was distracted. But the aeromancer whipped up a whirlwind of dirt, and while the swirling air failed to penetrate Ronan's shield, enough of the dust fell through that I was essentially blinded. Not being able to see right now was a death sentence. I flung myself sideways onto my good arm, attempting to throw off anything aimed or coming at me through the dust, and turned my focus on the aeromancer instead.

Stop.

The dust cleared just enough for me to dodge the next attack.

Aurelis and Ronan were much closer now. Was it just me, or were my partner's wings laboring more than usual? As if fighting Metcalf's influence was draining her strength.

Abruptly she angled her flight path toward me. And I had a sick premonition it *wasn't* so she could pick me up and get me the hell out of here.

I released Metcalf's stone and grabbed the pyromancy and speed stones instead.

Aurelis dove, her maw opening to show off her perfect ivory fangs and the fireball blossoming in her throat.

Oh *crap*. She was so big. So fast. Would the pyromancer's magic even stand up against dragon fire?

I was so transfixed by the fearsome, fiery death bearing down on me that I missed the guy creeping up from behind.

"Look out!" It was Strike's voice.

I spun. Stumbled. Fell.

Having supernatural speed didn't make me any more coordinated.

That fall saved me from the rock swung at my skull.

And then flames were all around me. Greedy and hungry and grasping.

They scorched the desert earth. And they scoured the flesh from the guy who'd tried to brain me with the rock.

My stomach heaved at the gruesome death. Another hostage I'd failed to save. First the man I'd murdered with my own hands. And now this one. His cut-off scream echoing in my ears.

But the power of the sentiment stone I clutched kept me safe. From the fire anyway.

Talons—long and sharp enough to rend my flesh like slow-cooked pork—raked toward me through the still-hungry flames.

I launched myself backward, knowing I was too late, too slow to dodge.

Then Strike was there. Flying into the ruinous flames to save me. To pit the momentum of her inadequate mass against the talons.

Her metal casing turned black, then red, then buckled under the heat. And when her weakened hull collided with Aurelis's claws, she fractured into a dozen pieces.

But she bought me the milliseconds I needed to evade the blow.

The flames died away as Aurelis swept past, already gaining momentum for a second attempt.

Leaving me to stare at the charred skeleton that had been a hostage mere moments ago, and the smoking wreckage that had been my personal protection drone.

How had I ever thought I could do this?

Ronan landed beside me on the scorched earth, a sword, edges carefully blunted, in hand. His grave yet determined face above his battle armor snapped me out of my stupor. My grief. My self-pity.

"You've got this, Lyra," he lied. Then lunged to defend us both.

Woodenly, I picked up the scrap of Strike's metal hull that had landed next to me. It was still red hot, but I was still impervious. I shoved it into my pocket beside the pyromancer stone and turned to rejoin the fight.

The rest of the incursion force arrived with a volley of gunfire. Gunfire that was all noise and no bullets, but the others didn't know that. Their numbers spread the lethal attention of Metcalf's protectors around and gave the mind-controlled Aurelis a host of new targets. Which in turn gave me a tiny bit of space to think, to plan, to do more than scramble to react.

But I couldn't rip the information we needed from Metcalf while Neyomara continued to protect his mind from magical interference. Nor could Metcalf take over mine while Ronan was shielding me from the same. Which created a sort of stalemate while chaos reigned around us.

So I focused on those I *could* still help. Focused on saving Metcalf's hostages from themselves.

My breakdown could wait.

I found the duplicate mage again and compelled him to create as many copies as he was capable of and have them run the bricks of explosives out of the combat zone—before stray magic could blow us all to smithereens.

Then I ordered him to run to safety. Run away. Why hadn't I thought of that sooner? Metcalf's magic had a limited range. If I could get them outside of it, he couldn't re-ensnare them.

I sent the same compulsion to the others I could see, one at a time to make sure it overpowered anything Metcalf had them doing. Striving to clear the area of all but the incursion force personnel who were on my side by default—until or unless Metcalf managed to split his attention away from Aurelis to change that anyway.

But having Aurelis under his control gave him an ace card that was hard to beat. And my heart ached for my proud and lofty friend. For what she must be going through as she turned on her own colleagues.

All around me, magic and weapons and flesh and fire collided. People were dying. I didn't know how many. I only knew that for every scream I heard, there might be another who no longer had the capacity to scream.

We had to take Metcalf down to end this.

To save Aurelis, and to save others *from* Aurelis.

And to do that we had to—

"Ronan," I rasped. "Do whatever you need to do to stop Neyomara from shielding Metcalf."

Uncertainty warred across his face. He could keep up his magic shielding even if he left my side, but he couldn't protect me from a stray blade or bullet or talon.

"I'll be all right," I promised.

Still conflicted, he nodded and sprinted for Metcalf and Neyomara, his wings pressing the air for extra speed. I was alone.

Then Aurelis came at me again.

I grappled for her mind, guilt and revulsion spreading over me like oil over water. I hadn't wanted to do this. To invade her head. To violate her. But surely better me than Metcalf?

Right?

Except Metcalf was too strong for me to wrestle her away from him. Or I was too weak to overpower her mind at all.

Because she was on me in a heartbeat.

The pyromancy stone protected me from her flames. And I was grateful it was in my right pocket because my left arm was growing increasingly unresponsive.

But unlike the flyby attacks, this time she landed.

Her jaws snapped, and I danced backward, only my dad's supernatural speed saving me. Then I ran. Not trying to be heroic. Merely trying to survive long enough for Ronan to expose Metcalf's mind.

A fresh torrent of fire followed me as I fled, veiling her next attack.

Aurelis's tail lashed. Not in the playful way that I could usually dodge. It came hard and fast like a serpent's strike, slamming into my fragile rib cage and flinging me a dozen yards across the battlefield.

The agony of landing on my broken ribs and wounded left arm made my vision go dark.

And when the blackness receded, I wished it hadn't.

I'd landed right in front of Metcalf's feet. Which meant I could see his tight smile. His lack of fear. His lack of shame or regret. Lack of anything but the knowledge he was outnumbered, that he would eventually lose, and his determination to inflict as much suffering on me as possible before that happened.

Because Miles was also sprawled in the dust nearby.

Unconscious or maybe... no. His chest rose in a shallow breath.

My own chest wasn't working properly. I couldn't breathe. But not for any magical reason. Maybe I was winded. Or maybe a fragment of rib bone had pierced something it shouldn't. Or maybe my heart was so heavy with dread that it was pressing on my lungs.

Aurelis touched down beside my father.

My mind screamed at me to get up. To fight. To save him. But I couldn't move. Could barely curl my fingers around a sentiment stone.

No, dammit! Metcalf wasn't controlling me. This was my own body refusing to do its job.

The screams and chaos around us continued. I had failed. Failed to stop the bloodbath. Failed to save the hostages or the incursion team. Failed.

But I could not fail in this.

Distantly, I wondered whether Ronan would be mad at me for lying about being all right.

Metcalf's smile widened, and he flicked his fingers theatrically at Aurelis.

"Go on, my pretty lizard. Show Lyra what I do to the families of traitors." His gaze dropped to me, and he shook his head like a tourist lamenting his luck at the slot machines. "Traitors I had such great plans for too. Death would be too quick for you, little lyrebird."

Blood dripped across my vision. I hadn't even known my scalp was bleeding.

Desperate, I cast around for anyone close enough to

intervene. Anyone close and strong enough to save my father from my friend.

But I came up empty.

Aurelis was fighting Metcalf. I could see it in the strain of her muscular neck. The slowness of her wicked talons and teeth as they descended to rip open my father's chest.

Her great head jerked and angled toward me. But her talons were still outstretched. Still lowering toward Dad's prone form.

I readied my chain magic. But I already knew it was hopeless. I could drag Miles toward me. Perhaps make Aurelis miss that first strike. But then what? My fire magic was useless. My speed equally so when my limbs were so dreadfully heavy. And I'd already tried and failed to overpower Aurelis's mind. Right now I wasn't even sure I could convince my left hand to move the inch it needed to find the correct sentiment stone.

So I tore my gaze away. Felt a piece of myself die as I did so. And focused back on Metcalf. *Behind* Metcalf. Where Ronan and Neyomara were battling it out.

Neither of them was in the best of shape. Ronan had donated a significant amount of his blood and power to my father to wipe my memory only an hour ago, and all his magic was now reserved for shielding us both from mental coercion. Neyomara had been living outside of Faerie and spending herself to magical exhaustion for over a week.

Only one of them was trying not to kill. Only one

of them was fighting of their own volition. Ronan trying valiantly to keep her alive while she threw everything she had left at him.

Instead of using the chain to move my father, I sent it streaking toward Neyomara. Not expecting to actually succeed in my attack, only hoping to interrupt her focus, to give Ronan the opening he needed.

She saw the chain coming and dodged. But Ronan took advantage of that flicker of distraction. His wings flashed in a lunge, and his blunted sword smashed into her neck, magic sparking down the blade.

She went limp. Fell.

Ronan caught her before her skull could bounce against the bloodied dirt.

I did not hesitate.

My retracting chain yanked Metcalf's feet out from under him and dragged him down to my level while my stiff, unwilling fingers twitched up against the needed sentiment stone. I paid for that tiny movement, my entire left side flaring in sharp, blazing protest.

Then he was at my mercy.

At my bidding, his own magic compelled him to rescind his orders to Aurelis and everyone within reach.

And in that moment, as he registered the unpleasant revelation that my magic could now affect him, yet he still couldn't affect me, Aurelis spoke.

"Take his magic, Lyra," she ground out through teeth that had recently been descending on my father. "Please. Trust me. Kill the bastard and take his magic."

Horror flooded through me. In a mind and body so drenched in horror I hadn't thought it was possible to feel it anymore.

Not at the killing part. Some part of me had already made up my mind to kill him.

I believed in the law, in the justice system. It wasn't perfect, but without it, things would be worse.

But the justice system had already convicted Metcalf. Then failed to contain him.

How many lives had that failure already cost?

How many more lives would be lost the next time he escaped?

He was too dangerous to live.

But take his magic? Forever?

Everything in me recoiled at the thought.

Possessing Metcalf's magic permanently would spell the end of my life. Everything I'd been fighting to preserve. To hold on to.

The job I loved. The people I loved. The city I loved. They'd all still be there, but they'd no longer be there for me.

No way could a cop with that kind of power be allowed to exist. No way *should* a cop with that much power be allowed to exist. No one should have that much power. And if I did, who would ever trust me? Who would want to be in a relationship with someone that could take over their mind at any moment?

How could I even trust myself? Would the temptation wear on me over time? Corrupt me over time?

Would I nudge my little siblings to be quiet when I had a migraine? End a lover's quarrel with a thought? Force others to do my bidding because the end "justified" the means?

But Aurelis had earned my trust. And she'd done as I'd asked on countless occasions over the course of our partnership. In the past ten days alone she'd taken a volley of submachine gunfire to her scales, hacked into security footage, protected my secrets, and had my back or saved my life more times than I could count. I still found it hard to believe she'd allowed Ronan, a *fae*, the race that had once harnessed dragons as their personal beasts of war, to fly on her back.

Aurelis—who'd just become all too familiar with the torment this power could inflict—had asked me to take possession of it.

Hell, she'd even said *please*.

I gritted my teeth.

Metcalf's mind was vulnerable. Unprotected. And when he tried to move, I used my chain to truss him up like the pig he was.

Then I compelled him to speak.

Tell me where the threat to Washington is coming from.

His hands curled into fists. For all the years he'd used and abused his magic, he'd never experienced it from the other side.

It appeared he didn't like it.

"Missile Combat Crew Commander Ragowski," he

spat, "from the Mojave missile launch control center sixty miles north of Vegas."

I shouldn't have been surprised, but I was.

Even knowing a threat was imminent, the US defense force wouldn't have been able to stop it. Not launched from so close, from their own side. Instead of a handful of minutes' warning before impact as they'd have for an intercontinental missile, there would be only seconds. Instead of coming in over the ocean where there were specialized defensive installations that had a chance of intercepting it, it would come from one of their home-based missile silos.

And that single thermonuclear warhead—assumed as it no doubt would be to have been fired by a double agent of the enemy—would overcome other nations' "no first strike" policies and ensure that when the US president ordered retaliatory nuclear action, no one would stand in her way. And then all hell would break loose.

Praying the information would be enough to stop the impending devastation, I drew on Metcalf's magic again. The magic I despised. The magic he'd thrust upon me and forced me to use to kill.

He had honed me into a weapon.

Now I would use that weapon to take him down.

I let the chain fall away, holding him in place with my will instead. Then forced my uninjured arm to pass him something from my pocket.

Metcalf's head jerked around to stare at me as the

new compulsion hit him. Even now there was no fear in that remorseless gaze. Only hatred. Rage. Calculation.

He raised the blackened scrap of metal that used to be Strike... and slit his own throat.

My bloodthirsty drone would've liked that.

CHAPTER TWENTY-NINE

With Metcalf out of the picture, Aurelis back in her right mind, and my having easier access to his magic than I'd ever wanted, the fight fizzled out swiftly.

My dad was okay. A concussion and a fractured collar bone from when Aurelis had knocked him out cold earlier in the chaos, but he'd be okay. And the incursion team had brought plenty of medics to tide everyone over until they could be treated more thoroughly.

After his own once-over, my father regained consciousness and insisted on removing compulsions on anyone he could. Not everyone had been in range when I'd forced Metcalf to rescind his orders.

Another medic patched me up enough that I could hobble around with Ronan's assistance to round up the stray surviving hostages as well as any in the incursion team who'd fallen victim to Metcalf's magic too long ago to be reversed. No longer needing a sentiment stone, I persuaded them to go peaceably to the facility where they'd be held until the compulsions faded.

We had Aurelis to thank that so few of our people had been brainwashed. Her better-than-you-at-everything dragon superiority meant that keeping her under control had tied up nearly all Metcalf's concentration. And even *under* his coercion, she'd managed to pull her punches a little when it had mattered most. Which meant her presence was also probably why our final tally of casualties was low. Too high. But a lot better than I might have guessed.

Despite that, Aurelis seemed subdued rather than triumphant. She volunteered herself to patrol the area while the rest of us cleaned up, putting distance between us.

I worried for her.

I worried for myself.

And when she alighted beside me as I waited for transport to the hospital, it appeared she might've shared my concerns. Because she spoke two words I'd never expected to hear from her.

"I'm sorry."

I hesitated. The truth was I was a little uneasy around her after being on the receiving end of her wrath. But of course, it hadn't been *her* wrath.

I shoved down my discomfort and rested a hand against her warm, copper shoulder. "Don't be. I of all people know what it's like to be under Metcalf's control."

And her fighting so hard against that control was the reason my dad was still alive.

"Not for that." She huffed like I was an idiot for even thinking it, then lowered her voice. "I mean for asking what I did of you. To kill him and take his magic."

"Oh." My hand slipped a fraction. "Why did you?"

"We'll talk later. Not here. But I'll be out of town for a few days."

She dipped her head so her eye was level with mine. "So *try* to keep the wallowing and worrying and beating yourself up stuff to a minimum until I return, all right?"

Then she expelled hot breath into my face the way she often did as a show of disapproval or irritation. Except this time it was so gentle it felt like a caress.

I watched her fly into the night, immediately doing all the things she'd just advised me against.

By the time I was released from the hospital, Missile Combat Crew Commander Ragowski had been located and detained along with his crew. And just to be safe, the entire missile launch control center was going to be temporarily shut down and guarded around the clock by an all-new special-ops unit shipped in from out of state.

Washington was safe. And it was decided by people

far more important than me that we'd consider the matter settled with that. Something about having me attempt to override the G23 world leaders' compulsions being more likely to lead to an international incident than prevent one.

As for me, I received an award for outstanding service, a plainclothes cop who followed me everywhere in case Metcalf's compulsions hadn't been entirely erased by my memory loss, and an indefinite suspension pending a review I suspected may never come.

Which was how I was sitting in my apartment at one in the afternoon in my pajamas and regretting I had no ice cream left in my freezer. The sucky thing was, I couldn't even remember *finishing* the last of the tub. Had Strike thrown it out, or had I eaten it? I had no way of knowing.

Thanks, memory wipe.

Miles and the kids had returned from Faerie two days ago and were just down the hall. But I was reluctant to inflict my miserable mood on them.

It wasn't even that I minded the suspension this time. Not yet. I needed time to recover from the trauma and get my head on straight, and even I could figure out I shouldn't be in the field right now. I supposed that was why Gadson had *strongly* recommended I see a psychologist and stared me down until I took the proffered business card.

But despite having nothing better to do, I couldn't quite scrape up the motivation to call the number. In fact, I was struggling to find the willpower to do anything much.

Unfortunately, that meant the long day yawned ahead of me. Full of long, empty hours followed by long, restless nights where memories—some my own, some from Strike's recordings, and some conjured up by my brain trying to fill in the gaps—preyed on me in my dreams where I couldn't escape.

Things could have been worse.

None of the other things I feared had come to pass. Yet.

Miles, Aurelis, and Ronan all knew about the magic I now possessed and the horrible things I'd done with it under Metcalf's control. None of them were treating me like I was dangerous. Damaged. Untrustworthy. And my siblings had been told about my new magics and hadn't run screaming either.

But they didn't know everything. None of us did. There were times I'd left Strike behind. Times that she hadn't recorded. And those blank, unaccounted hours haunted me as much as the horrifyingly documented ones.

Dad had assured me it wasn't *me* doing any of those things. That I wasn't in charge of my actions and could no more be blamed for what I'd done than I'd blamed Stewie for dressing up in a devil costume and opening fire on pedestrians.

Dad had a good point. But my conscience wasn't convinced.

It was even less convinced that permanently taking possession of Metcalf's magic at Aurelis's behest had been a good idea. And I'd yet to hear from Aurelis any explanation that might give me reason, if not comfort, to counter that conviction.

For so much of my life, I'd wished I could've had a more powerful—or at least more acceptable—magic gift. I hadn't realized how small my concerns had been. How good I'd had it. That I would one day wish I could go back to worrying about the odd civilian complaint.

Now I had more power than I'd ever wanted. And it had stolen my chosen future from me.

But even so, I had plenty of blessings to count. I had family and friends doing their best to distract me, cheer me up, and support me—when self-preservation said they should be distancing themselves instead. And Gadson had made sure I had several months' pay to give me time to "pick myself up and find my feet." Even if the unspoken subtext of that was that I wouldn't be returning to the department.

I'd just decided to rewatch the entire *Brooklyn Nine-Nine* series for the fifth time when Sage let herself into my apartment. "Daddy says you have to come over right away."

I jerked out of my slouch. "Why? What's wrong?"

She smiled slyly. "Not going to say until you come."

Frowning, I decided my pajamas would do for a thirty-second venture into the outside world—all the way to my family's apartment a few doors down—and followed her to the front door.

Sage waited for me, her ears perked in anticipation, and reached for my hand. Hells. Her innocent trust and acceptance made me want to cry.

But I wanted to give her this happy moment even more. And it must have been happy because she started practically skipping as she hustled me down the hallway.

"We're going to watch a movie!" she announced.

I puzzled over that and was left no more enlightened than before. Watching movies was not something we tended to do as a family—because finding one that would satisfy the tastes of all involved was virtually impossible.

"And Uncle Ronan brought Faerie popcorn!"

I skidded to a halt, cartoon style. *Ronan* was there? And here I was still unshowered and wearing my pajamas. I tried to remember the last time I'd looked in a mirror or brushed my hair.

Or my teeth.

Sage's ears sank, and her dark, soulful eyes lifted to meet mine, full of anxious pleading.

"Aren't you coming?"

It wasn't even a toss-up. I decided right then that free will was a myth. Those eyes were far more compelling than any magic.

"Of course I'm coming."

And I let her tow me the rest of the way, her corkscrew curls dancing with every excited step.

Sending Sage must have been a strategic move on Miles's part. There was no better way to ensure I'd shove aside my blanket of misery and hotfoot it over there.

Blake and Archer rushed me as soon as I walked inside and demanded to play their new favorite game. It involved one of them standing on my shoulders or hanging precariously off me while the other took a photo or video in which I, using one of my three new magics, was conspicuously absent.

At least it meant my current state of slovenliness wouldn't be recorded.

Dad rescued me by announcing the movie was about to start, and I saw Ronan already seated in an armchair with the promised popcorn.

Was it him or the popcorn that made my steps and heart quicken?

"What are we watching?" I asked as my three younger siblings grabbed their individual bowls of popcorn.

Ronan and Miles exchanged a look, then gave me matching enigmatic smiles.

I harrumphed and sat down, trying to shield my own popcorn from thieving, sticky fingers.

The movie, it turned out, featured me as the starring heroine.

Which made Ronan the dashing hero.

Aurelis had apparently sorted all of Strike's surveillance footage into categories. And Ronan had taken it upon himself to put together a short film from the one labeled *Cringeworthy Courting*.

I gawked in astonishment as Ronan came into my apartment with a plate of cookies. We both looked as awkward as a pair of teenagers. Dad was snickering softly to himself. Archer and Blake were questioning Ronan about the sword—Archer about how sharp and heavy it was and Blake about its history and the number of people it had "granted passage to the afterlife."

It was harder to guess at Sage's thoughts. But she was snuggled into my side, and after barely seeing me for two weeks, I suspected she'd have been happy to watch a blank screen.

Then in the "movie," Ronan carried his mug to the kitchen, scanned the contents of my fridge with a slight shake of his head, opened up the freezer, and grabbed the ice cream. He shot Strike a wink, then tucked the ice cream not so discreetly under his jacket and glamoured it into hiding.

"What on earth?" I asked, spinning to face Ronan.

He was covering his eyes as if it hurt to watch. "It only gets worse from here. Consider this my penance for my part in your memory loss. I thought it was only fair you got to see the footage, but it was your father's idea to watch it with the *whole* family."

When we got to the part where Ronan walked me to my door after the ball, I didn't know whether to be relieved or disappointed we didn't kiss. In the end, I settled on relief. Even my younger siblings would figure out the subtext of *that* one.

The movie ended with corny music and some throw-together credits. When had Ronan found time to do this?

"What did you think?" Dad asked.

"Boring," Archer declared. "Can I play a video game now?"

"I liked the pretty dresses," Sage said loyally. "Lyra looked like a princess. But the armor would be better for fighting bad guys."

Blake shrugged. "The kelpie and Ronan's friend were cool. I've never met a dread wight."

I was speechless. So I bought myself time to think by running my finger around the popcorn bowl and savoring the last residue of butter and salt.

"I don't mind forgetting the rest of it," I lied. "But I can't believe I've forgotten what Ronan's Faerie cookies taste like!"

"Delicious," Archer put in helpfully.

"Wait, he made some for you too?"

My brother looked sheepish. "Um... I woke up and needed to pee and found them on the kitchen counter. I didn't know they were for you!"

This started an immediate debate over what was the best food they'd tried in Faerie. I sat there trying not to feel envious until Archer mentioned the crunchy bug he'd enjoyed in his fox form.

Ronan just seemed relieved the ordeal was over and

he was no longer the object of attention. He rose to his feet, graceful as always. "That reminds me, I asked Cade to do a final cook-up for you all before he left. Lyra, would you help me bring it up?"

"Sure." I leaped to my feet and followed him out the door before recalling I was in my pajamas.

Ugh. It wasn't like he hadn't noticed. I'd just have to hope the building gossip Mr. Goswami was otherwise occupied or I'd be fielding disapproving looks for weeks.

Ronan waited until we were outside by his car before turning to me. "It's only one trip's worth of food, really. But I have to get back to Faerie, and I wanted to give you this." He handed me a flash drive. "What we watched were just the highlights. This is everything. With and without me."

My fingers trembled as they closed around the drive. There'd only been time to watch the most mission-critical footage before we'd headed out to Devil's Hole. And just now I'd watched fragments of something that seemed more fiction than reality.

The blanks in my memory had been bothering me, yes. And this would fill in some of them.

But would knowing make the nightmares better or worse?

That said, I *was* curious about the rest of the minutes I'd spent with Ronan. Maybe I wasn't imagining the way he was looking at me differently these days. More... intently. Warmly. Like he hadn't had to work too hard at feigning attraction to me after all.

Ronan brushed my clenched fingers with his, throwing me a lifeline from the whirlpool of my thoughts.

"If you decide to watch it all and want company, you have my number."

CHAPTER THIRTY

Shored up by my family's love and Ronan's voluntary humiliation and offer of company, I summoned the energy to do two things I'd been putting off.

Well, five if you counted showering, brushing my hair and teeth, and getting dressed.

I made a phone call first, then brought the charred and dented remains of Strike's metallic body to Zax. The drone had saved my life. Saved Washington with the footage she'd captured. Maybe even saved the world. If her AI was still in there somewhere, she deserved to be revived.

No matter how many irritating questions she asked.

When I walked into the shop, Zax looked like she was considering taking *my* flesh as recompense for her destroyed prototype—perhaps directly off my bones with her pointed teeth. But her expression softened when I made my request, and softened further when I gave her the final unused sentiment stone by way of apology and partial reimbursement.

She promised she'd see what she could do.

Stewie was next on my list. I wanted to thank him in person, but I hadn't wanted to ambush him. Hence the earlier phone call. I'd warned him about my new magics and told him I'd understand if he would prefer to keep our conversation over the phone.

I braced myself for his answer, fully expecting him to cut all contact, ditch the phone, and maybe even leave the city. He had a history of paranoia after all, which had saved me from Metcalf's horrendous plans. But would now spell the end of our relationship.

Metcalf's magic, *my* magic, didn't require paranoia to fear. To avoid at all costs. *That* was the rational response to someone being able to take over your will with a thought.

But Stewie had only said, "You're still good people, boss. Figured that out the first time we met, and power doesn't change that unless you let it. Besides, how else will Zeus convince you to give him loads of treats?"

So of course I'd brought doggy treats. An entire shopping bag's worth.

Lucky it was Stewie's hearing that was superpowered rather than his sense of smell.

We met on a street corner. I greeted him as usual with a quiet "Hey, Stewie" and waited for them to emerge.

Stewie looked a whole lot better than the last time

I'd seen him. Or at least the last time I *remembered* seeing him—in a holding cell at the precinct. My heart lifted to see his cheerful grin and easy stride back in place.

As a rule, Zeus stuck firmly to Stewie's side like a dog-shaped shadow. But today he trotted a few paces ahead to greet me.

I smiled and crouched down to pet him. "Hey boy, nothing wrong with your nose, hey?"

Stewie's eyes widened when he saw the bulging bag of treats.

"Yikes, boss. You're gonna make him fat. Can't have a dog called Zeus gettin' fat. His namesake might get pissy and strike me down with lightning."

I chuckled. "Just as well I asked for the low-fat types then. There's kangaroo jerky and beef, um, pizzle"—I'd made the mistake of asking what part of the cow that was—"and peanut-and-pumpkin biscuits and all sorts of things in there. Healthy and delicious without additives or preservatives since I know Zeus doesn't like those."

Stewie shook his head, his ready smile still in place. "Sheesh. Spoil him any more and he might follow *you* home instead of me."

"Not a chance. You can't buy that kind of loyalty. Besides, we both know you're happier for me to spoil him than you." It was my turn to shake my head. "You really ought to get a pay raise. That's twice this month you've saved us all."

Stewie gave me a bashful grin. "Naw, boss, you're

giving me too much credit. You did all the hard stuff."
He selected a treat from the bag and tossed it down to
his little black shadow. "But Zeus and I could go for
some more of them fancy burgers with you if you feel
like grabbing dinner?"

I grinned back. "It's a deal."

I returned to my apartment with my own bags of
groceries and treats, feeling something loosely resem-
bling normal for the first time in weeks.

But my empty apartment—something I used to
enjoy for its peace and solitude—now felt lonely and
depressing.

Could I really have gotten so used to having a drone
around for company that it now felt incomplete without
her?

Or was this just another sign that I needed to call
that psychologist?

Either way, the empty apartment and the prospect of
another long night of unrestful sleep pressed in on me
until that bubble of normalcy burst.

I was eyeing the flash drive Ronan had given me like
it might bite when someone knocked on my door.

I flinched. For reasons I didn't quite understand.
Then went to see who it was.

Ronan. With his beautiful wings on full display and
a plate of freshly baked cookies.

I opened the door so fast I almost hit myself in the face with it.

"Are those for me?"

"Yes."

I'd seen my blissful expression when I'd tried them in the footage, and I was dying to shove one in my mouth and discover what all the fuss was about. But I also recalled my poor hostessing skills the first time he'd visited. "Can I get you something to drink? Or a bowl of ice cream?"

Humor glinted in his dark eyes. "I never say no to ice cream. I brought pomegranate cider for us too if you can provide the glasses."

He trailed me to the tiny kitchen made tinier by his presence.

I dug around for glasses and bowls. "You know you can get ice cream at the supermarket, right?"

"I'm aware. But you expressed great disappointment that you couldn't remember what my cookies tasted like. And I realized that was one wrong I could actually right." He paused, hesitating. "And I didn't like the haunted look lurking behind your smiles."

I set the bowls down on the counter and stared at him.

My dad had warned me to watch the quiet ones. They often observed too much.

"I don't get it. Why isn't everyone distancing themselves from me and my abhorrent power? Don't you realize how dangerous I am? What I could do?"

"Because they know who you are, Lyra. Know your character. Stars, even I know you wouldn't use your new magic unless it was for anything but the best and most selfless of reasons, and I've only known you for a few weeks."

"Wouldn't I?" I countered miserably. "Two weeks ago I would've sworn I'd never kill someone I could have spared. But four days ago I did."

That memory was plenty clear. Metcalf's cold gaze locked on mine as he lifted the piece of jagged metal I'd given him and opened up his own throat. Those eyes going lifeless as his blood spilled out and out, too much even for the thirsty desert soil to drink in.

"Two weeks ago you probably couldn't have envisioned being enslaved by a psychopath willing to kill billions of people for his own gratification either," he pointed out.

I closed my eyes, not having a good comeback, but not feeling a whole lot better either. "Maybe it's a slippery slope... I feel like I don't even know who I am anymore."

Ronan was shaking his head.

"You killed a psychopath who had no regard for the lives of others. A man who tortured you, who planned to enslave you, who'd laid all the groundwork necessary to annihilate the world, and had escaped the 'inescapable' new prison system once already. If you're really worried about it being a slippery slope, how many more of those are you likely to encounter?"

He released a slow breath. "Three weeks ago you were beating yourself up for saving a girl's life at the potential cost of countless others. Now you're beating yourself up for taking a life to save countless others. Sounds like the same girl to me."

I studied my shoes, trying to absorb some of the conviction I heard in his voice.

"I know your life has been overturned," he said quietly. "It doesn't mean it's over. We'll help you figure out a new one."

My mind flashed back to what he'd said about his parents in the footage we'd watched.

"When the old ways are crumbling beneath you, you can cling to the fracturing foundation with every bit of your strength in the hopes you can shore it up a little longer—or you can let go and jump."

Would I be strong enough to let go?

"Besides"—he sounded a little smug now—"*I* can protect myself from you just fine."

I grimaced, but found I could raise my head again. "I'm sure Neyomara believed that too. How is she by the way?"

"She's in fine spirits. Maybe too fine. She told me she wants a rematch and is threatening to pluck my wing feathers for having the audacity to knock her on her ass."

Despite myself, a small smile played around my mouth. "That would be unfortunate. I'm growing quite fond of your feathers."

His voice turned low and husky. "*Are* you?"

My body reacted to that bedroom tone with a rush of delicious heat, and the cookies abruptly seemed less important.

"Yes," I said, hiding my response to him behind a shield of humor. "I was thinking they'd be perfect for my sister's art project."

He jerked his wings high in protest, then slowly lowered them again, a frown creasing his forehead. "I… suppose she could have *one*."

I couldn't help it. I snort-giggled. "Ha! I was just kidding, but I knew she'd wriggle her way past your walls."

He moved closer to me, sidestepping the counter between us. "Actually, it isn't your sister who's gotten past my walls."

"Oh?"

He reached out and gently eased the spoons I'd forgotten I was clutching out of my fingers.

Oh.

"I like you, Lyra. And not just because you rub my parents' feathers the wrong way. Although that *is* an added bonus."

"Hmm," I murmured. "I'm afraid none of my fantasies involved your *parents'* feathers."

His eyes sparked with unholy interest. "Fantasies?" he breathed.

I leaned into him, raising my face to his. He was

already close, but I wanted to get closer. "Fantasies," I confirmed.

His gaze drank me in, sliding from my mouth to my eyes and back again.

"Like, can you imagine me with a pair of black feather earrings?"

Ronan's lips twitched. "Hmm. I'm afraid when I imagined my feathers against your skin, it wasn't your ears I got excited about." He extended a wing to trace my jawline with the tips of his silken feathers. Ending the sensuous caress at my earlobe.

My breathing hitched. And his lips curved into a full smile.

"I'm going to kiss you now," he informed me.

Then his glorious wings closed around us—and despite the fact my life was in shambles, my career toast, my dragon partner failing to return my calls, my power a beacon to FutureCorp and those who thirsted for it, plus a danger to everyone I cared about—the world faded to delicious black...

WANT AN EXCLUSIVE GLIMPSE INTO A DRAGON'S MAGNIFICENT MIND?
STRAP YOURSELF IN AND, WHATEVER YOU DO, MAKE SURE YOU'RE NOT EATING A BANANA.

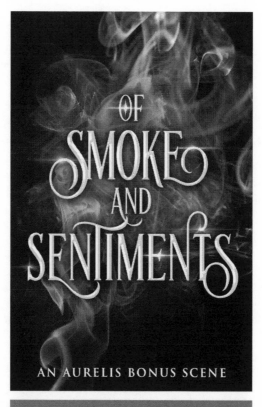

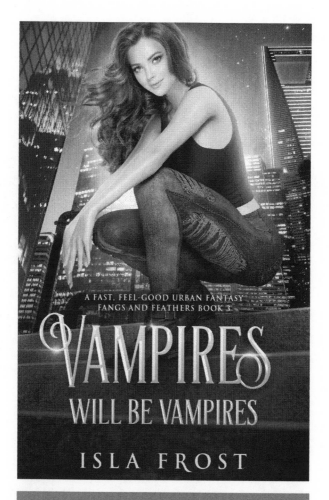

ABOUT THE AUTHOR

Isla Frost is the pen name of a bestselling mystery author whose first love has always been fantasy. She loves to write about strong heroines in fast-paced stories full of danger, magic, and adventure that leave you feeling warm and satisfied.

She also loves apple pie.

For updates and sneaky discounts on new releases plus occasional bonus content, sign up at www.islafrost.com

ALSO BY ISLA FROST

Fangs and Feathers Trilogy

Dragons Are a Girl's Best Friend

All Is Faerie in Love and War

Vampires Will Be Vampires

Firstborn Academy Trilogy

Shadow Trials

Shadow Witch

Shadow Reaper

Made in the USA
Columbia, SC
09 August 2024